ENES SMITH

COLD RIVER RUNNING

A Cold River Thriller

COLD RIVER RUNNING

Printing History
Enes Smith Productions

This is a work of fiction. Names, characters, places, and incidents either are the product of the author's imagination or are used fictitiously. Any resemblance to actual persons, living or dead, events, or locales is entirely coincidental.

Cover design by Duvall Design
Kindle Edition, October 2015 ASIN B011HTF0T1
Print Edition, October 2015
ISBN 978-1517580445

ACKNOWLEDGEMENTS

A special thank-you to: My son Tony, a deputy sheriff, with my admiration to protect and serve; daughters Melissa, Maddie, and Dani, and to my grandchildren, for their love and support; Retired Police Lieutenant Avex "Stoney" Milller, Warm Springs Indian tribal member, expert tracker, friend; Retired Police Chief Jim Soules, and friends, for putting up with my writing schedule and demons during a motorcycle trip; Donna Rich, for her skill and work to copy edit the manuscript; and Teresa Barrong, for her continued love and support, and courage wearing blue to protect our community.

AUTHORS NOTE

The probability of losing our electrical grid is increasing every day. We are a country at war and are vulnerable in so many ways. Our grid is a mish-mash of aging and new components, many of which are not made in the United States. Without electricity we cannot pump gas, deliver clean water, deliver food to stores, make purchases with credit cards, heat our homes, light our homes, have ice for cocktails, fly, drive to work, or have an operation. Our country might not survive a lengthy period without electricity.

Our elected officials know this and they have known this for a long time. Urge them to harden our electrical grid or face extinction via the ballot.

While this story is fiction, comprised of the author's imagination, work in Indian Country, work as a SWAT Commander, work as a homicide detective, and knowledge of human behavior – this story could be playing out in your community as you read this. Prepare for the survival of your family and neighbors.

William Forstchen's novel, "One Second After," is a thrilling read and possibly the most important book or our time. The book is centered on the survival of civilization after a bomb explodes in the atmosphere and the resulting EMP renders most electrical devices useless, including modern automobiles. Within a month of publication, I purchased a dozen copies of "One Second After" and gave a copy to each of my children, and to friends.

Faithful readers of my Cold River series will find old friends in Cold River Running: Chief of Police Martin Andrews and Lori Andrews; Smokey, Jennifer, and Laurel Kukup; Weasel, the pilot; elder Martha Couer d' Alenes; and Cold River Tribal Council Chairman Bluefeathers. You will also find new important figures: Nicole Kennedy, nurse, pilot, deputy sheriff; George Wolfhead, street gang leader who might become a tribal leader in time of need; and Jefferson County Sheriff Asher.

Cold River Running is the first of three books with the characters of Cold River, the central theme of survival after the failure of the electrical grid, and the need to go back to "old ways."

Finally, to my friends on the Confederated Tribes of the Warm Springs Indian Reservation of Oregon, thank you for continuing to read my work and your kind remarks. I am a *Šiyápu*, a white man, and as such, any mistakes I have made regarding Indian tribes, peoples, customs, and culture are mine alone. This is a work of fiction, from a *Šiyápu* looking in from the outside, and any relation to persons and events are from the author's imagination, and not related to real people and events.

Enes Smith
Metolius, Oregon
February 15 – October 2, 2015

DAY ONE

"March 22 will be remembered as the day of the electronic Pearl Harbor, the day we lost the electricity and went back to the Old Ways."

- Tribal Council Chairman Bluefeathers, Confederated Tribes of Cold River Indian Reservation of Oregon

"Only the dead have seen the end of war."

- Plato

Chapter 1

Cold River Indian Reservation of Oregon
Mt. Jefferson Whitewater River, March 22, 7 p.m.

Smokey would always remember this day as the day he saw the fox. The upside down plane and what came later was terrible, but the fox was magnificent .

The late evening sun made the snow gleam like a field of exotic pink diamonds, almost too bright for the human eye to take in. Smokey wore dark glasses, an invention by the *Šiyápu* (White Man) that he found useful. As the sun sat in the saddle of the mountain, the snow turned from pink to orange. Smokey was lying on the slopes of Mt. Jefferson, just down from White Water Glacier. He looked down at the trees in the valley, the green limbs of the pines covered with a heavy, spring snow.

Laurel, his ten-year-old daughter was next to him on his right, and his wife Jennifer was on his left side.

"Dad," Laurel whispered.

Smokey carefully glanced over and gave her a look. She was ten, but she had been with him in the wilderness since she was a baby, and knew that silence was a necessary stillness to see the *tuuptúup*, the silver fox. He raised his eyebrow. She should know that it meant to be still.

They had seen the fox seconds ago, and it had disappeared in the snow and trees, the valley shaded from the evening sun. If it meant laying here quietly for another hour, he intended to do so, if only for another look of seconds.

Mr. *tuuptúup* had suddenly appeared in the draw below them, careful, his nose testing as he drifted around a large Ponderosa Pine Tree. He had frozen behind another tree, this one within seventy yards, and had yet to reappear. Smokey waited. He sensed Laurel's movement as she began to squirm beside him. He would have a talk with her later. She had wanted to go with her dad on his trap line while she was on spring break, and now was acting like a city Šiyápu. Even his wife Jennifer, originally a city girl, was more respectful of the stillness.

Laurel shifted again, slightly, and Smokey saw her turn her face toward the sinking sun, ever so slightly. He was ready to give up on the silver fox and have some words for his daughter, when he saw the expression on her face.

"Dad!"

Several things happened at once. The *tuuptúup* flashed from around the tree and disappeared up the draw in a second's time; Smokey turned to admonish his Indian daughter, and she and Jennifer were both looking at the sky. Laurel pointed and started to stand.

Smokey looked up, and their day changed forever. A plane coming from the north, to the west of Mt. Hood in the distance, was on a path to take it directly overhead. It was a twin engine commercial airliner, a commuter plane from Portland, slowing in a normal landing pattern for the Redmond airport, forty miles to the south.

The silver fox forgotten, Smokey stood wordlessly, put his arm around his daughter, and reached for his wife. He had seen such things before, having served three tours in Afghanistan. Smokey Kukup, a Tribal Police Lieutenant, and his daughter, a tribal member of the Cold River Indian Reservation of Oregon, had never seen such things on the Rez.

The plane was upside down and on fire, trailing smoke and debris.

They stood and looked at the plane, and then when it went out of sight, they watched the smoke trail.

"Wow, Dad," Laurel said. Jennifer had her arm around her, reaching over to Smokey.

"Smokey," Jennifer said, "What do you think it means, those poor people on board, will it crash for sure?"

Smokey remained motionless and thought about the fox now. He had grown up on the reservation, had attended school in town, college down in Bend, and had served in the U.S. Army, mostly in Afghanistan, but he was tribal. He was an Indian, and as he thought about it, he knew that the fox had been a sign, a signal to them that their world was changing, more of a signal than the plane.

"It's going to crash huh, Dad?" Laurel asked. She was fixed on the smoke trail, and then turned to look up at her dad.

"Yes," Smokey finally said. "Inverted like that, with that much smoke and fire, I don't think they will right it and land. Madras is closest, but they were too high for that, hard to say how far they will go, off the reservation for sure. The smoke trail is well off the reservation, maybe over Lake Billy Chinook now."

"What do you think happened?" Jennifer asked. Smokey put his arm tighter around his wife. He could feel her uneasiness, her fear at the terrible sight, and with it, the fear of the unknown.

"I don't know, I've seen planes in such a way before, over in the middle east, but never here. There won't be a good ending. Whether this was caused inflight, or from something else, hard to tell now." He looked around at the terrain. "We should start back, this is not good."

"Dad." Laurel tugged on his sleeve and then bent down to put her snowshoes on. She spoke as she was fastening her bindings. "Dad, what do you think the fox has to do with this?"

The question from his daughter didn't surprise Smokey, nor was he curious about it. Jennifer would not understand it, but she didn't grow up on the reservation. He loved her with all of his being, but Jennifer was *Šiyápu*, a white. His daughter Laurel was born to be a *Twixtli*, a shaman, and as such, she had the ability to see things others did not. He should have realized that she would make the connection immediately, maybe before the plane.

"Something," Smokey said. "Something, for sure, and we won't know it for awhile, I think, maybe not for a long time." Laurel nodded.

Smokey helped Jennifer fix her bindings, stepped in his snowshoes, and kissed Jennifer on her cheek. She was not from the reservation, and he liked to do things for her, especially since she was six months pregnant. She smiled up at him, and leaned up and kissed him back. She was just over five feet tall and Smokey had been kidding her about getting round with the baby.

"Lead off, my husband," she said.

Smokey walked in the lead. His long hair was braided in a traditional way and moved across his back as he walked. Jennifer was next, and Laurel coming along behind. They walked their backtrail along the ridge above the valley with the *tuuptúup.* Smokey didn't look down. The fox was long gone, of that he was sure. They had a half mile to go, and stopped twice so Jennifer could rest. As they came up on the last ridge just above their truck, it was almost full dark, the twilight making it easy to see. Laurel stopped and pointed.

"Dad, what do you think?" Did the plane do that?"

Smokey and Jennifer followed her arm, looking down the valley, across the forest, and off the reservation.

"What?" Jennifer asked. "What do you mean, Laurel?"

Smokey knew what she was pointing at. He stood with them and looked across the valley. From there they could see for fifty miles. The lights were all off. Where there should be lights on in the town of Madras, and the neighboring towns of Metolius, and Culver, it was dark. They should be able to see the glow of lights from Bend and Redmond, with an area population of over a hundred thousand. Nothing. He turned to look back over his shoulder at Mt. Hood to the north. By now the night lights for the ski runs should be on. They were off as well.

The world was dark.

"I don't know, Laurel," Smokey said. He didn't think so. This was something else. There were no electrical substations for the plane to hit in the vicinity.

This was something else entirely. And their world was about to change completely.

And the *tuuptúup,* the silver fox, told them about it.

Chapter 2

Madras, Oregon
7 p.m.

"They're good," Lori said.

"I wouldn't take you off the reservation for just any band," Martin said. He watched his wife as she listened to Countrified, his favorite band. They had just finished dinner and Mark Mobley, the lead singer, was into his first set. The band had just returned from a gig in Nashville, and had announced that they would be playing in their old lounge, The Central Oregon Bar and Grill, a place where they started. Local country boys with talent.

Lori flashed him a smile and turned to watch the band again. She moved her head to the music, her-waist length black hair flowing on her shoulders as she moved. Martin looked around the room, a habit born of a life as a target. They were at a table on the side wall of the lounge, across from a bar that ran the length of the room. People were coming in from the restaurant side, and soon there would be standing room only.

The band started another song.

"Dance with me," Martin said, putting his hand on Lori's shoulder.

"I don't dance, you know that, husband. Not to this anyway." She covered his hand with hers and looked at him. He put his cheek on hers and said, "Okay then, a slow dance, the next one, I'll just hold you."

She shook her head slowly, side to side, but she was smiling.

"You went to high school here, I'll bet you danced all of those years, so don't pretend you don't know how. You were on cheer, I know. You go to your Indian heritage when it suits you." He said it lightly, sometimes a source of amusement to him. Lori could be fierce, but she had a tender, loving side, along with a mischievous, devilish, fun side. She kept him thinking. Constantly.

She laughed. "You got me there, chief."

Mark started singing George Strait's "The Chair," and Martin held out his hand. "Now, before the floor fills up. Don't refuse your older husband."

"I'll show you 'older' when we get out there." Lori stood up and took his hand. She was wearing jeans, tennis shoes, and a white sweater. He had a jolt of emotion, unusual for him, as she led him to the dance floor. He put his arms around her, and she put her arms on his neck, and they swayed. And then the music stopped, as if someone had pulled the plug. They were close enough to the stage to hear Mobley mutter, "Son-of-a-bitch," and turn around to look at the band.

The room had gone dark, shadows created with the dim lights of the emergency lights on the wall.

Martin stood on the dance floor and kept his arms around Lori. He looked over her shoulder and realized that they were all waiting for the lights to come back on, for the electricity to never fail them, as always. A man in his twenties, wearing a cowboy hat, came in the front door and made an announcement.

"Hey, folks, the lights are out all over town, can't see anything all the way down Fourth Street, up the hill too."

Everyone started talking at once. Martin moved Lori closer to the bandstand, a parody of dance without the music.

"Nice dancer, husband." Lori smiled.

"You ain't seen nothing yet," Martin said, and then to Mark, "So now what?"

"Well, hell," the bandleader said. "We were going to try some new songs out on you all tonight. Guess now we'll just drink." He laughed, and then grew serious. "What do you think, Chief? You know the town has two electrical providers, never seen it all go dark at one time, even in the Columbus Day storm."

"I don't know," Martin said. "I'm sure we'll find out soon enough. You be careful, Mark."

The crowd on the dance floor was starting to disperse, and some people were leaving. Martin waved at Jane, their waitress. She moved from table to table to get the patrons to settle up. He removed a fifty from his wallet and handed it to her as she walked by.

"This should cover our meals, the rest is yours," he said. She smiled and nodded thanks and walked to the bar.

"Maybe we should go, husband," Lori said, and took his hand. As they moved to the door, Martin heard yelling from outside, and they stepped out on the sidewalk. Gary

Henderson, a local math teacher, was standing with a group of people at the corner, pointing up to the south.

"Jesus, look at that," he said. He saw Martin and yelled, "Come look at this, Chief."

Martin and Lori got to the corner and Martin tracked Henderson's arm. He was pointing over the hill to the southwest of town. A commercial airliner, the twin engine kind that was used for commuting from Portland and Seattle to Bend, was trailing smoke, on fire, and upside down. In the darkening sky Martin could see fire coming from one of the engines, and what looked like fire on board. That would be Hell for the poor people. The sight was quieting for all of them, even those with a lot of booze inside.

Henderson's wife had her hand covering her mouth, shaking. She leaned on her husband.

"You think EMP, Chief?" Henderson asked Martin.

Martin pointed down Fourth Street. "Not with the cars running," Martin said.

There were cars in both lanes on Fourth Street, a one-way, two-lane state highway running through town, heading south. A line of cars, lights on, approached the intersection. The traffic lights were out.

An SUV, a big one, came fast from the west and wasn't slowing. A mini-van entered the intersection from the north, and Martin just had time to pull Lori back from the sidewalk when the SUV slammed into the van and knocked it up on the opposite sidewalk, the SUV spinning around and coming to rest in the middle of the street.

"Jesus!" Henderson ran to the van and yelled for Martin. Lori sprinted across the street as the rest of the cars came to a stop. She was trained. She was a police officer for the Cold River Tribal Police Department. Her husband Martin, a Šiyápu, was the chief of police. Martin turned to Henderson's wife. "Call 9-1-1."

When he got to the van, Lori was waving to him. She was half in the car, talking softly to someone.

"We have three people here, check on the passenger in front."

Martin looked into the broken, smashed passenger front window. A young woman was slumped head down, held in the seat by the harness, her head a mass of blood. He touched her neck to feel for a pulse, and found none.

"I can't get through," Henderson's wife said.

Martin looked up. "Have one of those people there run to the ambulance, just past Cliff's, three blocks that way." Martin pointed. Lori looked at him with a question. He shook his head, no.

"Martin, help me," Lori said. He turned back to her and she guided his arm inside the backseat area. "Hold this arm, a pretty good bleeder, I'll help Henderson with the driver.

He heard a siren, and then they had help. The medics took over. He stood up and walked with his wife to the corner. A black Chevy Tahoe came to the curb and stopped. Sheriff Jimmy Asher got out and walked over. He looked to Martin as he always did – a crisp starched uniform, nothing out of place. He had been sheriff for many years, but he always looked as if he were fifteen years old.

"Martin. Lori." He waved at the car, the intersection. "I don't know what we have here, but one of my deputies told me that the power was out all over. You see that plane?"

"Yeah. We did."

The sheriff's radio was going constantly. He leaned down to listen to his lapel microphone. "Shit."

"What's going on?"

"Some people trying to smash and grab at the Thriftway Market." Jimmy waved and got into his car. "If this calms down, let me know what's happening on the reservation." Martin nodded.

Lori was pulling him away. "I think we should go home, husband. Back to the reservation. There will be trouble there, I think."

They got to their pickup and started north on Fifth Street. The police radio in the pickup was going nonstop, set to scan all central Oregon channels. Lori selected the Cold River emergency communications channel, and picked up the microphone.

"Chief Andrews is leaving Madras for the Rez," she said. Lieutenant Kukup came on immediately.

"Chief, I am inbound from the mountain ... and boss we heard a report that the power was out all over, Portland, Seattle, all over. Meet at the PD?"

Martin started to answer, wondering just what the hell was going on. How could that be, power out all over? Lori tugged his arm and pointed. He looked to his right and saw a swarm of people running out of the Safeway store, and then heard a shot. He slowed.

"Nothing we can do, husband," Lori suggested.

Martin pushed down on the gas again, and left the scene behind.

They approached the Deschutes River, the boundary between the State of Oregon and the sovereign nation of Cold River. The Cold River Indian Reservation was a land of six hundred square miles on the eastern slopes of the Cascade Mountain Range, a land of forests and high desert country. The reservation was a land of rivers and lakes, and home to four thousand tribal members. Located seventy miles southeast of Portland, the Rez was a jewel about to be under siege.

Things were not any better on the reservation - not by half.

Chapter 3

Cold River Indian Reservation
J100 Road

"Smokey!" Jennifer held on to her shoulder harness with her right hand and braced herself with her left hand on the dashboard. Laurel was in the backseat of the four-door pickup, a grin on her face.

"Good going, Dad," she said calmly.

Smokey drove hard, putting the pickup into corners at the edge of control on the dirt logging road and at a speed that neither the pickup nor the road had been designed for. The police radio was busy with urgent calls, both on the reservation and off. He had talked with Martin Andrews and learned that the chief was on his way back to the reservation. *Martin will arrive at the police department before we do*, Smokey thought. We still have a long way to go, and all of it on old logging roads. What he had seen and heard worried him a lot more than he let on to his wife and daughter, although Laurel had the gift of knowing what people were thinking, feeling.

They were in the trees and on this part of the mountain they wouldn't be able to see cities even if they had electricity. The cities to the south were dark. The only lights they could see were from cars. The fact that they couldn't see anything to the north was even more frightening. Portland was on a completely different power grid. It just didn't make sense, but with the power out over much of the state, along with the plane on fire, that was bad. From their elevation in the daytime you could see over a hundred miles, especially lights after dark.

His first thought was that some of their enemies had set off a nuclear explosion in the atmosphere and the resulting Electromagnetic Pulse had knocked out all of the electronics and power. He now discounted that thought – he saw too many car headlights. His pickup and his radio were both working. Jennifer's cell phone was working, but she hadn't been able to get through.

"I'm going to the department," Smokey said, as he entered another corner. "I want you two with me until we figure this thing out."

"Dad, what about *ala* (grandma)?"

"Grandma has lived without power for much of her life. She will be fine, out there by the mountain."

Smokey, Jennifer, and Laurel lived in a large log house with his mother fifteen miles north of the town of Cold River, in a meadow just below Mt. Wilson, up toward Portland on the Rez. The area was wild, just out of the trees, and the house had kerosene lamps, a wood stove in the kitchen and the living room. It was as self-sufficient as you could get.

"If this is a long event, we need get some organization tonight. Both of you can help, and will be safe at the police department."

"It's going to last a long time, Dad," Laurel said in her matter-of-fact voice.

Smokey glanced at his daughter as he drove out of the trees. On this side of the mountain he should be able to see lights from most of central Oregon. It was dark as far as they could see to the south. Bend, Redmond, Madras, all dark, with an area population of two hundred thousand people, as well as all of the little communities surrounding them. They could see the housing areas of the Cold River Indian Reservation, and they were dark as well. They rode in silence, Smokey slowing the pace somewhat. They hit the pavement five miles out from town. The houses and ranches they passed were mute.

"A light in that house, Smokey." Jennifer pointed off to their right at a ranch house on the bank of the river.

"Kerosene," Laurel said.

Smokey glanced at Laurel. "*Ksla* (daughter), what are you thinking?"

"Dad, I see a lot of dark for a long time." Jennifer put her arm around Laurel and pulled the girl into her.

"I was afraid of that. Keep this between us, okay?"

Laurel had the gift of the *Shaman* as some tribes called it and Smokey had resisted it, denied it, and had warned his mother to stop helping his daughter learn the old ways. Now he wasn't so sure.

"Sure, Dad. " She gave him a wry smile and Jennifer laughed. "Does this mean I can talk to you about it?"

Smokey looked at her and turned his attention back to the road. He loved his daughter fiercely, and would protect her with his life, but sometimes she was so challenging. He nodded his head.

By the next morning he thought that he would have rather been ignorant of what was to come. It was going to get darker than any of them could imagine.

Chapter 4

North Los Angeles County, 7:30 p.m.

"It looks like a magical kingdom," Nicole said. She leaned forward in the left seat of the helicopter to get a better look. The rotors of the Robinson R44 helicopter swirled above them, the lights of greater Los Angeles below them and to the south taking up their entire view. The night flight was going as planned. Leonard Mitchell sat in the right seat, carefully watching his student pilot fly the craft. They had taken off from the Santa Paula airport at twilight for a ninety minute flight, the first at night for his student. Nicole was progressing as expected, and she was now in control of the Robinson four-seat helicopter. They had gone south toward LA, and were now heading north and east to leave the lights of LA County behind, to get into the dark countryside. Here the night was almost as bright as day. The ocean began as an abrupt line of darkness, spreading to the west.

"You could name the freeways with the lights," she said, excited. The helicopter dipped, and she corrected. "Oops, sorry."

Len smiled, and kept his tone neutral. "We don't have 'oops' when we are in command of an aircraft." She gave him a glance and concentrated. He answered her statement. The freeways were like ropes of lights, crisscrossing the land below them.

"Make a gradual turn to a heading of 240, and increase altitude to 5,000 AGL (above ground level)." Len watched as Nicole concentrated on flying.

They were turning toward the dark part of the land to the east, and increasing their altitude. He was the first to see the land go dark behind them.

What the hell?

A big section of central LA had suddenly gone dark, as if someone had shut off a light switch. Suddenly to the south, the south county went black, and then as far as San Diego, the lights were switching off, one by one, big sections of the land below. The lights to their left, Simi Valley and the area, just went out. Fucking out.

"My aircraft," he said, the hair rising on the back of his hand.

"Wha -?" Nicole swung her head to look at Len, and slowly removed her hand from the T-bar cyclic control. He gently moved the cyclic to bring them back around and look southwest toward LA and the Long Beach area. He glanced at Nicole, the craft swaying to his input. She leaned forward and put her hand to her mouth, her sudden movement causing a slight sway.

The freeways were still ropes of light, but the rest of the land was dark. It was one thing to have a power failure, but this was different, and they both instinctively knew it. He could see airliners stacked up with their landing lights on, coming into LAX from the south, looking like a string of lights up into the sky. He turned his radio on to the tower, and caught some of the traffic.

" I don't know, Delta 568, power is off in the area, but we are on auxiliary. You are still cleared to land, on runway ..."

He could empathize. He had been a pilot of a Boeing 737 until last year, and now had his own flight business. He missed it some, but not on nights like tonight.

He turned the R44 to his right, north, and kept the turn input so they swung to the east. Nothing but the lights of cars. He nudged the control and they swung back to the north.

Nicole found her voice. "What do you think, Len?" She was a trauma nurse for Santa Barbara Cottage Hospital in her day job, and volunteered as a Ventura County Reserve Deputy. She was used to emergencies, just not at five thousand feet.

"I don't know, probably not an EMP, or we wouldn't be flying, and most of the cars would be stopped. I don't know, but this doesn't seem local." He handed her his cell phone. "See if you can find a radio station on my radio app, and if it's working, find a station in San Fran or Denver or some other place. I'll figure out where and how to land."

"Can we land?"

"Yes, we'll go back. Even if the runway lights don't activate, I will be able to land. We'll circle around and look for the best approach. I have night vision in the bag in the back, was going to have you try them, but now we get to use them for real. We'll get down, alright, just don't know what we'll find when we land."

Nicole pulled his bag up to her lap, careful to not hit the T-bar, and pulled out the NVD bag. “In a minute,” Len said, “Take them out and hand them to me.”

He flew north into the darkness. They both saw an explosion on the freeway to their left, the 118, Len thought.

“Holy shit, what the hell was that?” Nicole pressed her face against the glass.

“Gas truck, I guess,” Len said. “Hand me the goggles, and when I say, take the T-bar.”

“You sure?” Nicole didn’t seem so confident now. “This is the stuff we train for, right? I trust you, and just use a gentle hand, keep aircraft straight and level. You can do it.”

“Okay,” Nicole said. Len held his left hand out. Nicole carefully held the goggles up so he could see them, and Len took them.

“Your aircraft,” he said.

“Got it.”

Len released the control and put the harness over his head. He adjusted the straps, and turned the device on. The night became day. “

“My aircraft,” he said, and Nicole let go.

It was eerie to see the dark houses, the occasional car, and the missing streetlights. They should be able to see Santa Barbara lights, an area of a half million people, and there was nothing. Dark.

Len slowed the R44 and dropped down to a thousand feet as they neared the 126 freeway. There were still quite a few cars there, and he would use the lights to guide him close.

"There's the runway," Len said.

"Not fair," Nicole said. "I don't have night vision."

"Dial the radio frequency in for the runway lights," Len said, "And when you get it dialed, activate the mic." Nicole had done this before. The radio on the right frequency would activate the runway lights.

Nothing.

"I was afraid of that." Len slowed more, and brought their altitude down to five hundred feet above the runway. No lights on the buildings either. He came down over the south end at a hundred feet, and found the darkness unsettling. He hovered near a hanger, and then closed the distance. He wanted to get as close as he could. He settled the R44 down to the side of the large doors, and shut down the engine. As the rotor spooled down, he tipped the goggles up and looked at Nicole.

"Well, we're here. Let's make our way to my hanger and figure out what to do from here."

"Fine by me." Nicole unstrapped and opened her door. As the outside air rushed in, they both heard a volley of gunshots from some distance away, to the south Len thought. Nicole turned and pulled a bag from the backseat.

"You got a gun in that thing?" Len asked.

"Yep."

They walked quickly to the pedestrian door in the hanger and Len opened it with a key. He instinctively turned on the light switch, and felt stupid when nothing happened. He motioned Nicole inside and shut the door. With his night vision on, he saw that everything was as he thought. His Cessna 172 sat in the hanger. He had a feeling they would be needing it to get the hell out of Dodge, or LA in this case.

And they did. If anything, the gunfire increased.

Len got a small generator going and set up two work lamps in the hanger to the side of the plane, worried that the light would be seen from the outside, but he needed to check the plane.

"You know the owner?" Nicole asked, and "This is nice, looks new."

"I own it," Len said, and opened the left door. Nicole followed. She was putting a holster with a Glock on her hip. Len started through a pre-flight procedure. Nicole followed, watching.

"You going on a trip?"

"Yes. As soon as I can, maybe start an hour before daylight."

"Really? Where?"

Len pointed to the insignia on the side of the pilot's door. There was the word "Weasel" and three teepees with feathers below it.

"What's that?"

"That is the Cold River Indian Reservation of Oregon logo. I have a place there."

"You Indian?" Nicole said as she followed Len to the front where he checked the three-bladed prop. "Hell, I thought you were from Central or South America or something."

"Weasel." Len said as he walked to the door. He pointed at the name on the door. "My name is Weasel."

Nicole turned to face him. "Weasel." She said it normally, and Weasel thought she was trying the name, the sound of it. She didn't sound disrespectful. She leaned closer, the lights chasing the shadows from her face.

"Before you can say no, listen to me." She spoke low, urgently. "My only cat ran off two months ago, and judging from what we are hearing from outside," she waved at the hanger door, "I don't think there is a chance in hell I could make it to the hospital, fifty miles away. If the power remains off in LA, it's going to be anarchy."

"But," Weasel said, "I don't think ..." He actually hadn't thought this far ahead.

"Look," Nicole said, keeping her face close. *She's not letting me out of this, Weasel thought.*

"Look, I'm a forty-one-year old divorced woman with no kids and I don't want to be left here alone to fend for myself. I would rather help you out on the trip, and I can do that. If you're worried about mileage, I don't weigh much. Let me go?"

Weasel smiled, and watched as the tension slowly left her face. He leaned back and tapped on the door of the plane.

"One condition," he said, smiling.

"What's that?"

"Weasel. My name is Weasel from now on. I'm a tribal member of the Cold River Indian Reservation of Oregon, and we're going to fly to my home."

And they tried to do just that.

Chapter 5

Cold River Indian Reservation

Martin and Lori were quiet going down the grade toward the Deschutes River. The only lights they had seen were cars and an occasional truck. The highway was busy.

"Why so many cars, husband?" Lori asked.

"I think the power is off in the casino, the Šiyápu can't gamble, heading home to Madras, Bend." She laughed. There was a steady stream of cars. As they got to the river, the Rainbow Market was dark, but the parking lot was full. *People trying to stock up on beer and wine*, Martin thought.

They saw the lights as they hit the new bridge. A Cold River police car was on the reservation side of the river, its overhead lights making red and blue flashes in the darkness. Smokey slowed, and then stopped in the road.

Officer Larry Wilson walked over to his driver's door.

"Chief, Lori."

"Power out all over?" Martin asked.

"Yep. Sergeant Lamebull told me to monitor the bridge. I've just been sitting here, watching the cars. Our radios work, though."

Martin nodded.

"Chief?" Officer Wilson had a worried look, unusual for him.

“Yeah?”

“Is the power really out all over? Dispatch has had reports of power out in Portland, Seattle, California.”

“You know more than we do, Larry, but we will let everyone know. If it is, it’s going to get ugly fast, I think. You be careful, let us know what is happening here at the entrance.”

“Chief, can we keep the bridge?”

Martin and Lori laughed. The Tribal Council Chairman had blown the bridge to isolate the reservation in the past, and after a long construction period, the bridge had been replaced.

“I don’t think it will come to that. You keep your head down. We’re going to the department to see what we need to do.”

Officer Wilson waved and walked across to his car.

“Actually, that wasn’t funny, keep the bridge,” Lori said. She chuckled as she said it, and then grew silent as they entered the parking lot of the police department. The lights were on in the building. The department had an emergency generator that was tested every month by protocol, and would come on automatically when the power went out, to provide instant 9-1-1 capability. Lori pointed at the lights.

“How much propane do we have for the generator?” she asked as they parked.

“I don’t know, guess we’ll find out tonight.”

An officer left the building and ran for a patrol car. He opened the door and yelled at Martin. “Shooting in the west hills housing.”

"You have enough people?" Martin asked.

"Three."

"I'll go," Lori said, and yelled at the officer. She grabbed a gear bag from the pickup.

Martin put his arm out and slowed her down when she trotted back. "You sure? Pregnant and all?"

"I'm only three plus months, husband." She gave him a warm, loving look. She lowered her voice and said, "Indian women have been pregnant and fighting for centuries, husband. I'll be fine, they can use me."

Martin knew she was right, no matter how hard it was for him to see her go.

"Go."

Lori put her lips together and mimicked a kiss, and ran for the car.

"Call if you need more," Martin said, rather lamely, he thought. The officer turned on his siren and accelerated out of the lot. Martin heard another siren from down below. He shook his head and entered the police department.

It's starting, he thought. He just couldn't have imagined how bad.

He entered the hallway and waved at the darkened window that separated the dispatch center from the public. The door to the police administration area clicked open, and he walked in. Jaime, his secretary was at her desk. This was not unusual for her. She always had a knack for showing up during emergencies.

"Hi Chief." She tilted her head toward dispatch. "You might want to go check with them, they have some information that is pretty bad."

"Thanks." Martin walked around the corner and opened the door to the dispatch center. There were two people at the radio consoles. Sheila Lenwa raised her hand and talked quietly, urgently on the radio.

Martin waited until she looked up again. She pointed at a chair next to her.

"Chief, I need to fill you in on all of the hell that has broken loose in the last hour." She motioned to her partner, and took her headset off.

"People have been calling in with reports, people who still have land lines in their homes, mostly the elders, telling us that the electricity is out all over the west coast, some say all over the country. We've had shots fired all over the res."

What else is new, Martin thought.

"Have you heard from Smokey?"

"He's on his way in from the mountain."

"Tell me what you know."

"We are on the emergency generator, and that runs dispatch, a couple lights in the jail and some computers/outlets in the admin and patrol areas. Electricity is off all over the reservation. And Chief," her voice quavered, and then she went on. "Chief, we have bulletins from 9-1-1 centers in Portland, Seattle, California, and east, like Denver – the power is out all over. Do you think we are being attacked?"

"I don't know," Martin said. He thought that they might be under attack, but kept that to himself for the moment. "We don't think it is an EMP since the cars and radios and computers are running. Sheila nodded. "What about a sunspot?" Sheila asked.

"We would have heard and been warned," Martin said. "It takes over three days for a Coronal Mass Ejection to reach us, and we would have been ready." They had studied the effects of a CME when they were getting ready for an EMP attack, as part of their county-wide readiness for disaster.

"No," Martin said, "this is something else. This was probably planned. What else do you have?"

"We have had a run on the gas station and they closed. People have been outside the market demanding that they open, and it wouldn't surprise me if people broke in tonight, panic and all. Officers are on a shooting in the west hills, but you know that since Lori is there. They are Code 4, by the way."

Code 4 Martin knew, was the universal police sign for "We're okay, no further assistance needed."

"Sheila."

"Yes, Chief."

"Can you get more people in here to help tonight? I think it's going to be a long night. I will find a way to call out everyone we can. Every time an officer arrives here, send them to me in the patrol room, and when you get enough help, I want you there as well."

He left and walked to his office, to find a very worried Jaime and two officers waiting.

Sergeant Lamebull and Officer Hoptowit.

"Come in," Martin said. *It's starting, and we have to start running now.*

"Sergeant, I want you to find a way to get every officer, every former officer, and the natural resources crew to the police department within the next hour. Get a list from Jaime," she nodded, "and send runners, people in cars, everyone who drives by to find these people and meet here in …" Martin looked at his watch. "Meet in the conference-room in one hour. Go." Lamebull turned and left. He was a large man with almost waist length hair, worn traditional, and a trusted and experienced officer who had grown up on the reservation. He would make it happen.

"Chief." Sheila stood in the doorway. "The facilities guy, Dave Houligram, says that we have enough propane to run the center for maybe forty-eight hours."

"Thanks, Sheila." To himself, Martin made a note to find more propane.

He turned to officer Hoptowit. "Jim, will you round up some help and check some things for me?" Martin didn't wait for an answer. "Take someone with you, doesn't have to be another officer, a relative, friend, but check on the gas pumps up on the highway, down at D&D repair, and up at the tribal motor pool, and the federal fire protection area. We are going to have to guard them sooner rather than later. Oh, and check on the store."

"I'll get my brother, he's just down the street."

"Fine, and when you check those areas, figure out how and where we can guard them from. The Shell station on the highway we may have to write off."

"Chief." Sheila was at the door.

"We are getting reports of fights on the highway, up by Mt. Hood."

"Nothing we can do about that now," Martin said, "but keep me posted." *We might have to close the highway soon,* Martin thought. *And that would lead to a war. One we have to be ready for .*

Smokey came in, with Jennifer and Laurel trailing behind. Martin motioned to the chairs in his office. Jennifer and Laurel took seats, Smokey stood.

"Power's off all the way past Bend," Smokey said, "And Mt. Hood is dark."

"It's probably worse than that," Martin said. "It might be out all over the country."

"I thought so," Laurel said, matter-of-factly, and they all looked at her.

"Well, just saying, I think it's off all over, and what's worse, I think it will be off for a long time." She shrugged. They didn't argue with her. Smokey gave his daughter a long look, and turned back to Martin.

"People are going to get mighty hungry," Smokey said, looking at a map of the reservation as he said it.

"We have a lot to do in the next twenty-four hours," Martin said. "Smokey, I want you to be on top of our position tactically. You have the most experience with warfare, and I think it might come to that, protecting the Rez from an influx of people trying to stay alive. And it could get ugly. Come up with a plan to keep the peace on the reservation, and to defend this country from the outside."

"Chief," Sheila said from the doorway, "We have people trying to break into the IHS." IHS, Martin knew, was the Indian Health Service clinic, with a full pharmacy of meds. Shit!

"Send who you can, and then find someone to guard it. Call Hoptowit and Lamebull, and have them devise a plan with trusted friends and relatives to maintain a guard on the essential services that Hoptowit is looking at. As soon as you can." Sheila left and trotted back to the dispatch area.

Martin leaned over and rubbed his eyes. He knew he was forgetting something, a lot of things, and he just hoped that it wouldn't get someone killed.

"Smokey, can I get an accounting of our armory, weapons, and especially ammunition? Also, devise a plan to form a militia, and who would be in it. Do we have a list of former military?"

"Weapons and ammunition I can get in two minutes. I've been thinking about your last request, and I believe we have some talent here with regard to military and experience. I expect we could field a couple of platoons within a week. Raw, but organized with some pretty good leadership. Hell, Judge Wewana was a combat Marine, as well as Chairman Bluefeathers."

Martin raised an eyebrow at that. He did not know that Bluefeathers was a veteran. It did make sense, the chairman's sense of warfare, of right and wrong.

"Bluefeathers was a combat marine in Viet Nam, saw a lot of action early in the war, leading up to the Tet offensive."

"Well, that explains a lot," Martin said.

"Chief." Sheila was in the doorway. Martin looked up.

"Chairman Bluefeathers is here." ***The God comes a'calling,*** **Martin thought.** ***The one in charge.***

Chapter 6

Simnasho, 7:45 p.m.

Traditional Tribal Community, thirty miles northeast of the Cold River Agency

Tribal elder Martha Couer d'Alenes carried a candle lantern out to her barn to look in on her cow and her old sorrel mare. She had just finished milking her Jersey cow when the lights went out. She didn't mind the power outage and didn't know that the power was out in any other place. The power went out often in this traditional community in the northern part of the Cold River Indian Reservation. On the slopes of *Pàtu,* or Mt. Hood as the whites called it, Simnasho was a collection of houses, a store, a fire and safety station with an engine and ambulance, a church, and a closed school house. The most important building in this community of two hundred was the Simnasho longhouse, a meeting place for weekly events, a place for festivals and celebrations. Each year, the Simnasho longhouse hosted the Lincoln Pow-wow in honor of the sixteenth president of the United States, and brought hundreds of Indians from reservations around the country.

Martha had been thinking about the root and berry festival, a celebration for the traditional way of gathering food. She knew that one day it would be important for the people to learn the old ways, and as much as possible, she lived the life style of the old ways.

Martha's house was an old two-bedroom farm house, built before WWII, and had received upgrades from the housing people every so often. It was set back a third of a mile from the center of the small community, up on the edge of the tree line. The small barn behind was at the edge of the trees. *Pàtu* rose up behind her. She walked down the worn path from the barn to the back porch and opened the screen door. She stepped out of her rubber boots and into a pair of deer-skin moccasins and entered the kitchen. She put the candle lantern on the counter. She had what she called her little country kitchen, with an ornate wood cook stove on one wall. She started a fire, and when she was certain it would go, she moved a kerosene lantern to the counter, and lit it. She turned up the wick and the light of a sixty watt bulb chased the dark from the kitchen.

A thumping on the front door startled her. No one came out here at dark. She carried the candle lantern to the door and opened it.

"*Ala*, open up." The voice was her grandson, Gopher. Indians had given names which were rarely used on the reservation. Her grandson lived down at the Agency, twenty five miles away, on the edge of the reservation, down toward Madras. "*Ala!*′

Martha opened the door and Gopher stood there, breathless. He had just left high school last spring, and was working in Tribal Administration, studying to be an accountant. A good boy, even if he did drive too fast. He took Martha to town to shop a couple of times a month, and she always chided him for his driving.

He wore jeans, tennis shoes, and an Oregon sweatshirt. His hair was long, now an okay thing for In-dins to do again. He had rings in his ears. All in all, a good boy.

"What is it, Gopher?"

"*Ala,* the power is out."

"Come in, *Pusa,* (grandson) and slow down. What are you trying …?"

"*Ala,* no, the power is out all over, I mean even in L.A. and Portland and all over. What do you think? People sent me to ask you, thought you would know. And Dad sent me to check on you."

"Let me see, *Pusa.*" Martha looked out the front window, down toward the longhouse, and couldn't see lights. There was always a light on the corner of the longhouse. The town was dark. Even the fire and safety station was dark.

"Grandson, when the power is out here, it doesn't matter if the power is out all over. It's just out. I think those Šiyápu in the cities might have some problems, but it is always the same here. The power goes out, we go back to the old ways for a time, and then the white man's power comes back on." She moved into the kitchen, where the fire in the kitchen stove was going along nicely. It would be about thirty degrees tonight, and the kitchen wood stove would do just fine.

Martha went back to the front room and opened the door. Her grandson trailed her and stood in the doorway behind her as she walked into the front yard.

Martha looked down the slope to the town. The longhouse was dark, and across the street the ambulance station was as well. Three Feathers store and service station was dark, but she could see the headlights of some cars there. A loud exhaust sound came from near the store, and a motorcycle flashed by, it's pipes resonating off the trees. *It's the Teewee boy*, she thought.

The Simnasho resident tribal police officer had a lamp on in his home, down across the road. His car was gone, probably going to an emergency out on the highway from Portland. From Martha's place, she could look over the high meadow at the intersection down by the store. The Simnasho highway ran below her, and continued to the Cold River Agency and town twenty five miles to the south. At the store, there was the confluence of the Wapinitia Highway and the BIA Highway 3. The BIA highway ran north for thirteen miles through high mountain trees and meadows to the northern part of the reservation. South from the store, the Bureau of Indian Affairs highway went for fifteen miles to the Kah-Nee-Ta Resort. Simnasho was a collection of houses with about two hundred people and was the most traditional of communities on the Rez. At one time Simnasho was the seat for Indian government. It's isolation was extreme – they were literally in the middle of nowhere. They could go for days in the winter storms before the roads were plowed by the Bureau of Indian Affairs road crews.

At times Martha was active in tribal government, and would often make the trip to Cold River several times a week to take part in planning, in festivals, and to ensure that the Simnasho residents had a voice in what was going on down there. She helped serve traditional food in the tribal jail, and thought that the *Siyapu* police chief Martin Andrews was a good man. She had even given her blessing for the crazy one, Lori, to marry him. There were many in this traditional community who didn't want the *Siyapu* on the reservation. Martha would scold them when she heard such talk. She knew that they needed the whites. She knew what was in Martin Andrews' heart. She knew that he was a good man.

She felt a chill and started to go back into her house when she heard the sound of voices coming from the store. Loud. Angry. The harsh noise of breaking glass, an unmistakable sound like the warning rattle of a snake, came up to the slope to them. Martha's grandson looked at her.

"Come inside, grandmother," he said. His voice said more to Martha than anything he could have told her. He was shaking. He was scared. She put her hand over his and stood her ground on her little porch. More glass breaking, and then a gunshot. They both jumped at the sound, and then a flurry of shots, ending with what Martha was sure was a shotgun blast.

"Aaiieee." The yelling continued, and then stopped. Two cars left the front of the store with tires screaming, and flew up the Wapinitia Road away from the store and out of sight. A third car accelerated away, flashed by the fire and safety building, and then on the Simnasho Road below Martha's house.

"That's Tanisha's Blazer," her grandson said.

Martha nodded. She wished her other grandchildren safety tonight.

"Let's go in now," she said, moving to the screen door. She had seen and heard enough. She waited for her grandson to close the door.

"Pull the drapes," She said. She walked to her bedroom and removed a case from the top of her dresser. She brought the case to the kitchen and went back to check on the drapes. She didn't want any light to escape from her house. This kind of thing had happened before, but not this fast, and she knew in her heart that this was going to be bad, maybe the end of the reservation and her people. She would need to sit and think about it.

She took the wooden case into the kitchen and placed it carefully on the table. It was the size of a computer bag. The wood was old, and had scratches and some writing on it. Her grandson looked on.

"What is this, *Ala*?" She looked up at him, and realized that his world of cars, cell phones and friends was about to change. She knew that she would have to stay alive to be the voice they needed. She wasn't a demure, wilting flower like some of the new age In-din women were. She was a leader, a strong woman, and she knew what must be done. She opened the wooden box. Gopher leaned over her shoulder, and then stood up and turned to look at her.

"*Ala*, what is this? It looks old, like a museum piece."

Martha reached in the case and picked up a heavy revolver. In places the bluing had worn off, and the metal shined, as if recently oiled. "It's a Smith and Wesson revolver, and your grandfather carried it when he worked for the tribal police, in the fifties."

"*Ala*, are you sure that thing will work?"

"This will work for the next hundred years. The only enemy of this gun is rust and politicians, and I keep it oiled and away from politicians." She smiled, and opened the cylinder.

"Ala, do you even know how to use it, to shoot it?"

"Don't be smart, boy, of course. Your grandfather and I used to shoot all kinds of guns when we would go into the woods to pick berries and dig roots." Martha Couer d'Alenes picked up a box of shells from the wooden box, swung the cylinder open, and started to load her revolver. She smiled a grim smile.

"Won't be people breaking my windows, *Pusa.*"

They didn't know then just how soon Martha Couer d'Alenes, an eighty-six-year-old tribal elder, would be needing her husband's revolver. And her knowledge of the old ways.

She sat the heavy gun down and saw Gopher watching, his eyes bright and watchful.

"You know how to shoot, Gopher, you and your friends grew up hunting. Why does it surprise you that your *Ala* has a gun and knows how to use it?"

"I don't know," he said, shaking his head. "I just never thought of you that way. And *Ala,* don't you think we should get in my car and head down to the Agency? We could make the twenty-five miles in twenty minutes, the way I drive." He grinned.

"I think, grandson, that we won't be comin' around using the road. That road will be for death plenty soon enough." She went into her bedroom and called to

Gopher, holding the lantern up, the shadows dancing on the walls.

When he entered the bedroom she pointed at a shelf.

"There, get those two canvas bags down for me, grandson."

When he placed them on the bed, she opened them and folded two blankets and placed one in each. "For our travel," she said. They both jumped as a series of gunshots came from down by the Three Warriors Market.

"Grandma, Ala, what do you think?"

"I think we pack some things, saddle the mare, put a harness on the cow, and get ready to go."

"Uh, grandma, go where?"

"To the woods and make our way down to the Agency."

"On foot?" He looked horrified.

"Yes, we used to do it, a long time ago, your grandfather and me."

"Ala, how long did it take you, a month?"

She gave him a look that was short of a fool, and said, "No, Gopher. It only takes a day and a half, and that's staying off the roads."

"Take this bag to the kitchen table." When he got the bag there, she was pulling supplies out of cupboards. Two tin cups, two bowls, spoons, a knife and sharpener. As she had Gopher reach for matches and candles, they heard a single shot.

Gopher raised his eyebrows. "What do you think it means, Ala?"

They both listened, standing still in the kitchen. The sound grew louder, and then the roar of a truck vibrated the windows. Gopher slipped into the dark living room and pulled the drapes back an inch.

"*Ala,*" he said, his voice in a whisper, as if they could hear him down on the road. "*Ala,* there are cars down there." He walked slowly back into the room and stood by the kitchen table. Even in the soft light of the lantern, his grandmother could see he was worried. Scared.

"I think it means that we pack in a hurry, and put this stuff on the horse, and put a harness on the cow. We are going to have to leave in a hurry."

Neither one of them could know just how bad it would get before the day ended. But this was Simnasho, and what could happen here?

Chapter 7

West Hills Housing

"Turn your head away from me!" Lori gave the order and walked through the living room toward the man. He wore jeans and boots, and no shirt. He was lying face down, handcuffed with his hands behind him, and he was smiling. He had a large tattoo covering most of his back, and Lori knew from experience that it was a tattoo made in prison. The tattoo was XV3, for 18th Street, a member of the 18th street gang, originating in L.A. The gang was known for its violence.

"Why don't you come here, puta, and make me."

Lori moved fast, and Officer Kyle Lakala moved across the room to assist. She held up a hand, stopping him.

"Don't look at me, George!" She yelled and dropped a knee into his back, forcing the wind out of the gang-banger. She reached down and turned his head. He tried to get his breath, making a whooping noise, and when he finally could, he wheezed, "Gonna get you for that, bitch."

"Stand in line," Lori said, and stood. That's all they needed tonight. A gang shooting, and the likely shooter was on the floor in front of her. George Wolfhead, the leader of the 18th Street Gang, had shot a member of the Native Gangsta Tribe, or NGT. Wolfhead was muttering, and Lori could make out, "Got that NGT mutha fucka."

"Yeah, right. You can go back to federal prison, get some more tats." Lori kneeled down next to Wolfhead, and spoke so only he could hear. The other officers in the room were interviewing other gang members, their women.

"You're getting a little old for this, aren't you, George? You gonna die in prison, being the big 18th Streeter on the cell block. Why'd you do this tonight, huh? You could have had someone do this, you are the leader. WTF, George?"

"NGT can't be here," George wheezed, still trying to get his breath.

"Well, the NGT banger ain't dead yet, maybe you will just go for a gun charge and attempted murder. Should get out in, what, twenty?"

She stood up and motioned to Kyle. "What do you say we get him over to the jail, clear this up. Something tells me we are going to be busy, don't need any more of this gang shit tonight."

They stood Wolfhead up and led him outside. The evening had cooled off, the stars so close it looked as if you could touch them. The house was like the others in the housing district. Large half-acre lots, some even had grass, most with rusted out cars and appliances. The rimrock surrounded the valley. Lori had grown up here, but tonight she didn't have time to enjoy the beauty.

"Watch your head," she said nicely. She had known George most of his life, but that didn't mean he wouldn't try to kill her if he could. The gang culture was alive and well on most Indian reservations. Tribal members like

George were sent to federal prisons for violent crimes committed on the reservation, and became immersed in gang culture. They then brought the culture back to the Rez, along with a desire to increase the drug trade.

"It's my calling," George said with a smile. "Say, how's that Siyapu of yours. I heard that you two were going to make a kid."

"He's good, George." Lori turned to look at George as Officer Lakala got into the car and started it down the hill. "Say, George, how about working some of your time off?"

He smiled, thin, not friendly. "About how long do you think I would last up there in Sheridan Federal Prison as a known snitch?"

"You have a point, George."

It was eerie riding down the sagebrush covered hills, no lights on anywhere in Cold River. Some windows showed candles, others the light from kerosene lamps. She looked over at the modern Tribal Administration building. It was a large building with cedar siding and a blue metal roof. It housed payroll, benefits, HR, the Tribal Council chambers, and a host of other offices. She realized that she had never seen it dark in her lifetime. There were always lights on somewhere in the building, and the parking lot was usually lit.

They came around the corner and stopped at the four way stop. There were two cars parked across the street in the parking lot of the D&D repair, an auto repair and gas station. Martin must have already put guards on crucial services.

Kyle Lakala turned the Ford Crown Vic onto Hollywood street, and drove up to the BIA building that housed the police department, the 911 center, and the jail. There was a single light on in the front, powered by the generator no doubt.

"Sally-port won't work," Lori said. The garage type door for the jail entrance ran on electricity, and she doubted if it was hooked up to the generator circuit. She was right. The remote in the car didn't open the large door. They would have to do this the old fashioned way.

They parked behind it and Lori got George up to the pedestrian door, where they were met by a corrections officer. "I got him. We'll be right in. Thanks."

"Yes, thank you, Lori," George Wolfhead, the shooter said.

Lori turned around and said to Kyle. "A minute?" He walked ten steps away and watched. Lori nodded. She leaned in close to Wolfhead.

"Look, George. I don't know what's happening, or what's going to happen, but for old time's sake, we went to school together, for God's sake, what are going to do when the electricity stays off? Be in jail? Use your head. You're one of the smartest men I've ever met. Now you're running what? A bunch of gangbangers who couldn't hit their buttholes with both hands."

He turned to look at Lori and smiled, the tats on his face moving. "You sure are a hot woman when you talk dirty, you know that? Now you bumping that Siyapu. That any good?"

“Keep me out of this, George.” She moved her face closer to his. This might not work at all, but if they were truly out of electricity for a long time, things were going to change in a hurry. Tonight.

“If this electricity stays off, you going to have to figure out where you want to be, in prison, or out helping.” He gave her a strange look, and shook his head. No.

“Just saying,” Lori muttered, and motioned to the jailer.

George turned to look at her one more time as he entered the jail.

Chapter 8

Sandy, Oregon, near Portland
7:30 p.m.

David Allan Coe screamed through the speakers – "*Where bikers stare at cowboys who are laughing at the hippies, who are praying they'll get outta here alive.*"

The fact that you could smell the urinal from the front door of the Sandy Hitman Tavern was fine with Norman. In fact, it suited him. This was his kind of place. Most passersby would rightly call this a biker bar, or a dive bar. Norman Pierce, known in prison and biker groups as Abnormal Norman, drained the beer glass and slid the empty down the bar. He wore his usual uniform for town – dirty jeans, a black T-shirt, and his jean jacket vest, with a skull on the back. He didn't belong to a biker group, although he was often mistaken for a biker member. He just didn't give a shit what people thought he was.

Norman knew exactly who he was, and unless parents had given up on their girl children, he was a parent's worst nightmare. And he was about to make that known. He had been watching the little whore and her friends in the corner booth. He would tell them what he could do for them. And if they were lucky, he would take them back to his shop. His own version of a clubhouse. Then the fun would begin.

Abnormal had prison tats on his face, neck, arms, hands, back, and stomach. When he was on the outside, out of prison, he didn't add color to his tats, he wanted the world to know how crazy he was. He liked his prison tats, fading blue and gray ink, the only colors that were available in prison and jail. The teardrop tats below his left eye signified a murder, and that wasn't the worst of it. The numbers "14" and "88" were prominent on his forehead, ragged block numbers that were impossible to miss.

The 14 signified a racist quote from Nazi leader David Lane, with fourteen words in the sentence. The 88 stood for the eighth letter in the alphabet, for HH, or Heil Hitler.

The bartender carefully placed another beer in front of Abnormal. He slid off his stool, his gut falling down below his T-shirt, and walked over to the booth. On his way, the juke box stopped, and the lights went out. The tavern, dark at best, went darker.

"What the fuck?" Abnormal stopped in the middle of the floor and looked out at the street. A skinny biker named Rosebud with long stringy hair and similar tats came up beside him and pointed.

"Street lights out." There was some lighting coming from cars stopped on the state highway in front of the tavern. Abnormal glanced at the girls in the booth, and walked to the front door, carrying his beer. He pushed the door open and stood on the sidewalk, Rosebud beside him. The lights were out as far as he could see. He heard a siren to the west, and they watched as a Sandy police car made its way through the traffic and flashed past, heading up and out of town toward Mt. Hood. Norman took a drink and headed back inside. It seemed darker in the bar now, and someone in the back had a flashlight. He drained his beer and ordered another. The girls were getting up to leave. Any other time, Abnormal would have prevented it, but he had to think. Mike, the skinny bartender, had just told them that he was through serving. He came around the bar and Abnormal wiggled his glass at him.

Mike nodded. He got another beer out from the case, and slid it down to Abnormal. The bar might be closed, but he wasn't stupid.

Rosebud came up beside him. "There's talk on the street that the power is out all over – Portland, Seattle, even Cali. What you think?"

"Clubhouse. I think we go to the clubhouse," Norman said, and lifted his bulk from the stool.

Another police car was making its way down the highway. "Be a wreck up there, maybe." Rosebud said. Abnormal nodded. He signaled to the bikes at the curb. Other friends and fellow ex-cons were coming out of the tavern. He walked to his Harley Road King and threw his leg over. There were about a dozen bikes on the curb with him, and the owners began drifting out. Abnormal started his Harley and let it idle until most of the others were ready.

They rode out of town to the east, a surge of power and noise, and when they got to Shorty's corner, they saw what the police cars were heading for. A line of cars was backed up for a quarter mile. Norman slowed, and then swung the Harley around them, knowing the others would follow.

A bread delivery van was on its side, the contents strewn across the highway. A mini-van with a crumpled front end was in the middle of the road, leaking fluid, and a small car, a Subaru, Norman thought, was in the ditch. The police were letting traffic through from the east. As Norman approached the officer holding his hand up to block traffic, Norman gunned the Harley and accelerated past, catching a word of what the officer was yelling.

"Assholes!" The officer said, and then they were past, accelerating on the four lane road, the forest on each side now. There wouldn't be any officers coming after them. Not tonight. *Maybe not ever*, Norman thought, *maybe not ever*. Three miles from Shorty's Corner, Norman turned to the right and drove up a gravel lane for a half-mile, and then turned into a large lot in front of an old warehouse and garage. The property had been owned by a biker, long dead, and the Speed Merchants had taken it over as a place to meet. When people thought of "clubhouse" many thought of a golf course clubhouse. This building and meeting place made the tavern look like an upscale restaurant. You didn't need to be in the front door to smell piss at this place – you could smell it as you rode up. Broken down vans, cars, Norman's 4X4 Chevy.

Norman parked his scooter and some of the group drifted up. "I'll get a lantern going," Rosebud said, and entered the warehouse.

When they were assembled inside, the propane lantern hissing on the table, Ziggy handed a bottle of Tequila to Norman. He took a long pull, the liquid burning as it went down, and handed it back.

"Listen up," he said, and the room went quiet. "If the power is out all over, and doesn't come back on, we can't stay here. Not enough of everything."

"Who did it, you think?" A voice from the wall asked.

"Ragheads, be my guess," Norman said. A murmur went up around the room. "I want for us to spend the night gassing up rigs, some 4X4's, our scoots, getting food, water, all the guns and ammo we have, and we'll leave before dawn."

"Where?"

"I know a little town on the northern part of the Indian reservation. It's about an hour to the turn."

"What if the Indians object?" Rosebud asked with a laugh. This drew a laugh from the crowd, as well as Norman.

"Fuck'm," Abnormal growled, and he laughed with them. "We'll just take it from them."

Chapter 9

Cold River Police Department
11:30 p.m.

Martin Andrews sat behind his desk and looked at the small Indian man seated at a table in his office. Tribal Council Chairman Bluefeathers wasn't very tall, but Martin had never thought of him as small. What he lacked in stature he more than made up for in presence, his ability to wield power. On the reservation, a sovereign nation within a state within a nation, the tribal council chairman was the president, the governor and the leader of congress all rolled into one man. Some said that Bluefeathers had the power of God. He wore his usual blue jeans, cowboy boots, and a western shirt. He had long salt and pepper braids that hung down on his chest, with ancient bead and leather work and feathers used to tie off the braids.

Bluefeathers was a former Marine (if they are ever former) and tribal police officer. For Martin to say that Bluefeathers was a friend would not be entirely accurate. Since Martin had gone to Peru to rescue the chairman's granddaughter Tara, and had risked his life to do so, Bluefeathers had decided to keep Martin as a chief of police, even if he was a Siyapu. And it didn't hurt that Martin was now afforded an elevated category within the tribe – he was now MIT, or married into tribe. No, Martin wasn't a friend – but he had the respect of the old man, and that was as important.

"Chief," Bluefeathers said in a low voice, "You think this is for real? That the power is out all over?"

Martin looked at the man, the dark wrinkled face, eyes that sparkled with intelligence. "Yes. our dispatch center has official reports from 911 centers around the country. The power is off in Denver, Phoenix, L.A., Eugene, Salem, Portland, Seattle. We have heard that the power is on in a couple of eastern cities, but for how long, who knows?

"If it remains out for longer than a few days, we will be in serious trouble, I think," Martin said. Bluefeathers nodded for him to continue.

"The first problem, and we have started to address it, is to protect our supplies of food, medicine, gas, propane, weapons, and our infrastructure." He made a mental note to send someone to protect the dam on the Deschutes River. The tribes ran a hydro electric dam in partnership with Portland General Electric, a dam that was capable of generating enough power for Cold River and the surrounding cities.

"What about the highway through the reservation?" Bluefeathers asked. "Have we blocked it yet?" The last time the reservation was under siege, Bluefeathers ordered the bridges to be blown up, and they had just been rebuilt in the last year.

"No, but we will have to consider it soon. We don't have anyone coming up from the south, from Madras and Bend, except for tribal members, but the traffic from the north, Mt. Hood, Portland area, is increasing. We have a couple of officers on the northern boundary, monitoring the traffic."

"Three million people in the Portland metro area," Bluefeathers said. His depth of knowledge never ceased to amaze Martin. But the leader was, after all, a person used to testifying before the U.S. Congress. "Many of them," Bluefeathers said grimly, "Many of them, if only two percent of them, decide that they need to get out of the city and head east, will mean sixty thousand people on the road in the next couple of days. We can't handle that."

"I've thought of that, and at some point soon, we will have to block it," Martin said. "What do you propose we do with the people on the forty miles of road from the northern end of the reservation, to the southern border, here in town?"

"We keep them moving," Bluefeathers said. He stood up and walked to the window, his reflection making the glass a mirror. He stared at it, and Martin had the thought that the chairman was actually looking out at the hillside.

"But," he said forcefully as he turned around, "We give them water and snacks of a piece of fry bread as we move them along. We don't let them off the road. If this world ever gets back to normal, we want these Siyapu to remember, to tell others how they were treated on their journey through the Rez. Many of our people don't like the whites, as you know, but we need them more than they need us in this day and age." Martin knew then with a certainty why this man was called *wiyana i,* or elder leader. A very wise man. Oh, this man had a temper, that was sure, but he was always thinking ahead. For the good of the tribe.

"We'll organize that at the meeting. First thing," Martin said. There was a light knock on his door, and they both looked at it as it opened a few inches. Jaime stuck her head in. "Doctor Semington is here." The doctor was in charge of the clinic, Indian Health Services, a modern clinic with an emergency room, examining areas, a dental area, a pharmacy, and a staff of nurses. It was referred to as IHS on the reservation.

"Send him in," Martin said. Semington, a tall bald *Šiyápu* in his mid-fifties, entered and Martin waved him to a chair. Bluefeathers nodded. Semington sat on the edge of his seat, and it reminded Martin of how hyper Semington always seemed. Martin knew that the chairman had a lot of respect for Semington, a career IHS doctor who knew all of the Indian families, and had a reputation for taking care of the people. Semington started without preamble.

"The clinic is guarded for now. We have our own small emergency generator going, we have to keep some of the meds refrigerated or we lose them, principally the medication for diabetes, and a few others. But, what worries me is that we are out of some kind of meds within a week, others, we may last a month. If this goes longer than that, it will get serious. We can last without power, but some of the folks will die without a resupply of meds."

Bluefeathers said one word. "Who?"

"Diabetics without insulin, the process will start slow and then speed up. People on blood pressure meds, chronic and severe cases, other heart patients, kidney patients on dialysis, there is a whole host of things we prescribe medicine for that can be life threatening. We will do what we can, and may have to set up a ward to keep people, but if this goes on, people will have to be taken care of at home."

Martin had a sudden thought. Bluefeather's wife was a type I diabetic. The tribal leader had probably figured this out, but to hear it must affect him, just the same.

"Get a list of what you need to Martin in the early morning. We'll send some officers into town to see if we can get some from the hospital," Bluefeathers said. His face didn't show any emotion as he said it.

There was a slight knock on the door. Jaime stuck her head in again.

"Chief, most of the people are assembled in the conference room."

Chief of Police Martin Andrews, Tribal Council Chairman Bluefeathers, and Doctor Semington stood and made their way to the conference room.

On their walk to the room, Martin thought that the three of them were planning the survival of a country, a sovereign nation within a state within a nation.

DAY TWO

"The *Siyapu* built the dams, harnessed the electricity, and killed the fish. We got along fine before the *Siyapu* arrived. If we survive, we will show the others how to live in the old ways."

- Chairman Bluefeathers

Chapter 10

12:30 a.m.

In the end, it took Norman several hours to get the Speed Merchants ready to go. He had Rosebud take a crew and two pickups back down the road to the store and clean it out, with guns if necessary. The bikes and the vans were gassed up, gear tied on, and Norman assembled them in the warehouse when the pickups returned.

People thought of his group as an outlaw motorcycle gang. Most of them did ride bikes, but Abnormal didn't give a fuck about biker groups, they were mostly pussies, as far as he was concerned. His peeps had all done time. They were a prison group turned out. The *Portland Oregonian* had once run an article on his group inside and called them "The Speed Merchants" for the large amount of crank they had sold and still sold from inside the prison walls.

Hence, The Speed Merchants.

Rosebud came in at a fast walk. "This power had better be out for awhile," he said in a rush, "because we just robbed the store at Shorty's Corner blind. Made them help load, with the urging of my pistola here." He pulled out a large revolver and waved it over his head. Norman slapped him on the back.

"Okay, we are going to a little place called Simnasho, a town in the northern part of the Cold River Indian Reservation, about fifty five miles from here. Geno?" Abnormal called over the group. Geno Scott held up his hand. He was the enforcer for the gang, the Sgt. at Arms. "Geno, you will lead the group of bikes, with Rosebud, then Mike and I will follow. I want the fastest rider in behind the vans and pickups. Any problem, you jump up front and let us know."

Geno waved.

"One more thing, if it gets in our way, kill it."

"What about cops?" Liz asked.

"Them too. We will be in The Welches Resort ten minutes after pulling out on the highway. All of us pull around behind the grocery store, with the vans up close to the liquor store. If it hasn't been cleaned out, we will."

"There's gonna be some good shit at the resort liquor store," Rosebud said.

This brought a few cheers and laughter from the group.

"Jaz and Brother Bob and Ruthless in the rear van, heavy guns if we run into trouble. We'll hit the highway slow and when you get out, flash your lights and we'll pick up speed. Same thing at Welches." He raised his hand in the air and made a circular motion with his finger, and the group headed for the bikes and vehicles, talking, the excitement building, doing something to take charge.

Abnormal Norman got on his Harley Road King and waited for Rosebud to start out, then the other bikes started, and they rode down the drive to the highway. He pulled out behind the two in the lead, the morning cold, and felt the power of twenty-two other bikes behind him. The power.

That's what it was about. There was not a force on this part of the earth that would and could oppose them. They would have their own town in an hour.

They idled along as the rest of the bikes and vehicles got out on State Highway 26. The vehicles heading East toward Central Oregon gave them a wide berth, the driver's with their families leaving the city as refugees had done since the dawn of time. In prison Norman had done a lot of reading. He had once read that once a person leaves their home to escape war or famine, they stood a five percent chance of survival. Once on the road, you were mostly dead. There was more traffic than he had thought there would be.

Rosebud raised his hand and signaled for the group to take the center lane, and then go on into the nearest opposing traffic lane. They wouldn't be slowed down by mom and pop and the kids going somewhere. The woods closed in on both sides of the four lane road, and within minutes, they were in the Welches resort area.

He shifted down as the group slowed, looking for the blinking light that signaled the turn before the little shopping center.

Shit. The light was out, of course. Rosebud made the turn, slow. There were people bringing items out of the store to his left, dark figures, looters. Just past the store, the lead bikes turned into the darkened parking lot at the back of the store. The liquor store was along the side, in an alcove. He followed the lead bike, his headlight making the few cars in the parking lot come alive with light. Rosebud pulled around and rode slowly back toward the front. Abnormal rode up beside him and shut his engine off. As the rest of the bikes came up and stopped, the six vehicles pulled into the lot one by one, the van in the rear. Two of the pickups pulled trailers. They stopped in a line by the alcove.

Mike jogged down the sidewalk with a shotgun held in his right hand, followed by Jaz.

He waved from the sidewalk and walked over to Norman.

"Store's intact. There is the steel grate on the door and windows. I'll take it out." He went to the nearest 4X4 pickup and talked with the driver. He waved the truck forward with the front end on the sidewalk, and ran a cable to the grate and signaled the driver. Norman laughed like a kid when the grate on the door snapped off. He waved at the group in the dark parking lot.

"Listen up, we take everything we can pack into the trailers and trucks. All of you carry, let's get it done."

As the human chain of ex-cons and the eleven women with them carried out booze in a seemingly endless supply, Mike brought a bottle to Norman.

Norman held it up in the light of the pickup. Johnny Walker Blue. Over two hundred dollars a bottle. He removed the cap and threw it away. The first swallow was smooth, and damn, it was fine.

He laughed and handed the bottle to Mike. He was going to be the Genghis Kahn of Central Oregon. Maybe the entire state. Plunder and kill. Start with a little town in the northern part of the reservation. Fuck'm. He laughed and reached for the bottle. He was gonna get some Indian women to go with Johnny Walker, whether they liked it or not

.

Chapter 11

Tribal Police Conference Room, 12:30 a.m.

The room was full, every chair taken, with people standing along the walls. Off duty officers, some with their wives or husbands, some in uniform, medics from fire and safety, workers from natural resources (some of whom were sworn police officers) and even a few security officers from the now closed casino. People were talking in low tones, and the talking stopped when Martin, Chairman Bluefeathers, and Doctor Semington entered. A tribal police officer seated in front on the aisle got up and motioned for Bluefeathers. The chairman took the seat, touching the officer on the arm as a sign of respect. Martin stood in front of the room. All eyes were on him.

"Thank you all for coming on such short notice." He looked around the room. Lt. Smokey Kukup was there with his wife, Jennifer, and his daughter, Laurel. It wasn't unusual for tribal members to include their family members in important meetings, meetings of survival.

"By now, most of you know that the electricity is off, not just here, but apparently all over the country."

A short Indian with long braids raised his hand. Chester Whinishut. A former mill worker, now a police officer. "What you think happened, Chief?"

"We don't know for sure. The power is off in most areas of the United States, with a few exceptions. Probably not an EMP, or we wouldn't be driving most cars, have cell phones or radios. Not a sunspot, or we would have had ample warning. My guess, and we have been getting reports about this, is that a coordinated attack on our power grid by unknown persons. Terrorists is our best guess."

"What about the highway?" The speaker was a young dispatcher, a woman with a family.

"We haven't decided whether or not to close it, or when. And," with this Martin smiled, "the decision has been made to not blow the bridges." There was a scattering of laughter around the room. Martin felt that if Bluefeathers hadn't been present, there would have been a lot more laughter.

"What about the whites? No offense meant, Chief."

"None taken," Martin said. Bluefeathers stood up.

"I think that now we need the Šiyápu, the white man, as much as ever. When this is over, whenever that is, we will be judged on how we treat them, and we won't survive if we are not fair. They are many. We are not, even with a sovereign nation." Bluefeathers looked around at the silent room. He continued.

"That doesn't mean we are going to let anyone run over us. We are warriors." The room erupted in applause, even the Šiyápu applauded, Martin noted. Bluefeathers sat down and Martin held up his hand to get some order. As he was thinking of what to say, the door burst open and a very bloody officer Baker entered the room. Sgt. Lamebull and Smokey moved to help him. He had blood on his face and down the front of his uniform.

They sat him in a chair and Jaime came in with towels. Dr. Semington came up with one of his assistants and kneeled to help him. There was a large cut on Officer Tom Baker's forehead that was pumping blood. As the doctor cleaned around the injury, he asked, "Can you tell us what happened?"

Tom took a deep breath, and started. "Jimmie and I were up on the highway, monitoring the traffic from the top of the hill, and went to check on what looked like a minor fender bender. Both cars were blocking the downhill lane, right at the passing lane. Well we walked up, there were four or five people standing next to the lead car, a Suburban. They were yelling at someone in the car, and when the man got out of the car, the fight was on. One of the men standing there slugged the driver and he went down. When Jimmie and I jumped in, I was hit in the face with something, and went down. Jimmie yelled at them and fired a shot in the air, and they backed off. He got me in the car and brought me here. I think he's on his way back with other officers to clear them out."

Sergeant Lamebull stood and motioned to other officers. Martin waved for him to continue, and they left the room.

"We have a lot of things to do tonight and early morning, and how well we organize will determine how we survive." As he spoke, other tribal members were arriving and found places along the wall.

"I'm going to write headings on the board. Jaime, can you take notes so we can refer to this later."

She nodded, ready with a legal pad.

He wrote on the whiteboard.

SECURITY

And underneath he wrote, “Lt. Kukup.”

“Smokey will be in charge of overall security of the reservation. He is a veteran officer, and has been in a war zone, Afghanistan, several times. He will call on many tribal members, others, to help with a rapid response team to trouble on the Rez. He will be in charge of weapons and munitions, and overall organization of a militia, if it comes to that.”

Smokey raised his hand.

“I’m going to go rapidly through the things we need to sustain life.” Under security, he wrote

WATER

“We need purified water, and I need someone to head up a team to make sure we have a supply to be distributed. We don’t need an outbreak of cholera. If this power outage goes weeks, cholera will kill millions.”

Robert David of Natural Resources raised his hand, and Martin wrote his name down.

FOOD

“How we acquire, store, and distribute food will determine our survival. We will need organized roundup of cows, horses, and organized hunting parties. We will need a large planting program, native fisheries industries, and many other things here. Who can organize this massive effort. It will take a lot of help and labor.”

Again, Robert David raised his hand. A man in his fifties, with traditional braids on his chest. If anyone could get it done, he could.

A voice from the back broke the tension.

“We all know how Bobby likes to eat!”

The room erupted in laughter. Even Bluefeathers was smiling.

Martin continued. He wrote MEDICAL, and then ELECTRICITY – POWER and went down a mental list, calling for help from the room.

FACILITIES

STORAGE

LIAISON

As he talked, people were coming and going, and if anything, the room seemed to be more crowded. Martin turned to look at the group. Police officers, medics, farmers, millworkers, families. As he turned back to the board, a voice came from the back of the room.

"What about the trucks?"

Martin turned back to the room. The speaker was Benny Tananowit, a large man with long braided hair. He was a logger, worked for Danny's Logging.

"What do you mean, trucks?" Martin asked. People were looking at Benny.

"Well, at any given time, there might be a hundred or more trucks on Highway 26 going through the Rez. We have thirty five miles of highway in this nation, State Highway 26 runs from north to south and we could conceivably keep all of the trucks here. Even at three trucks per mile, and that's a small estimate, we have over a hundred trucks at any given time, and we are letting them drive off the Rez, and they will just be commandeered by some asshole with a gun."

"What do you propose we should to?"

"Well, those trucks will be full of food, medicine, gas, diesel, propane – and someone at some point soon will take them. Let's just detain them, park them, in case this goes on for a long time. The drivers we let go, telling them that they could lose their lives if they drive off."

At the mention of gas, diesel, and propane, Martin looked closer at Benny. He was right, and a Safeway truck alone would carry a lot of food.

"Can you head this up, Benny?"

"Be glad too."

"Get with Lt. Kukup, see if he can give you two officers, one to turn the northbound trucks, the other to divert the southbound ones, say to the Rodeo Grounds."

Benny moved to the door. He had three of his drivers with him.

"You might have just saved us, Benny," Martin said as a way of thanks, and the loggers left the room.

Bluefeathers stood, and the room went quiet.

He walked to the front, and stood beside Martin.

"You know," he said in a quiet voice, "That this man, this man who married a tribal member, tamed Lori," and at that the room erupted into laughter again. "This man has done good by us, and we will use his skills. And I want to say something about his role, and other Siyapu. They are our brothers if they work here. I would like for those, tribal members, Siyapu, who have families off the Rez, to go now and keep them safe. If you can make it back here with them, you are welcome. I know some have already gone, and now is the time for the rest of you to go and check on your families." He looked over the room with a grave face.

"People are going to die, there is no other way, ot matter what we do. But we have to survive." The room remained quiet as people thought about what he had said.

"About the road. There will be many from Portland and other areas who think they will have a better chance on the road. That is false. If we get great numbers on the northern border, we will do our best to turn them around. If we have to, we will let them through, monitoring them, helping them along if they break down, but *NO ONE* gets off Highway 26. They move through. If it gets to be too much, we will close the border."

Elder Nancy Eaglewolf led them in a prayer, singing in Sahaptin and English. Several people stayed in the room to organize their work parties, and Martin made his way back to his office with Lori by his side. Smokey, Jennifer, and Laurel followed. As they made it to the door of his office, all hell broke loose. It was only four a.m. on the first night.

Chapter 12

Santa Paula Airport

Weasel and Nicole pushed the hanger door open in the dark. The door screeched, a sound that didn't seem so loud in the daytime, but now, with the possibility of people wanting the plane, Weasel winced at the sound. He was sure it could be heard for miles. He looked around at the darkened runway.

"Let's do it," he said. He touched Nicole's arm, and moved in the direction of the plane. Weasel opened the left side door as Nicole did the same on the right. When they were inside, Weasel started the engine, and the instrument panel came to life. He let it idle for a minute inside the hanger, the glow from the panel giving their faces a ghostlike visage. He hoped that anyone outside might not be able to pinpoint the sound. He slowly pulled the plane out of the hanger, and taxied to the south end of the runway, the night vision goggles giving the reflectors on the side of the runway a bounce of green light. He lined up the Cessna, turned up the power and held it, then released the brakes. A car came onto the runway, halfway down, running toward them. Weasel pulled the goggles up as fast as he could so the explosion of light wouldn't blind him and pushed the throttle in for maximum power. He felt Nicole stiffen beside him as they picked up speed and sped toward an almost certain head on collision. Nicole screamed as the car was right there, going to hit them head on, and Weasel pulled back on the yoke and they shot up over the car, airborne.

"I have a STOLL kit on the plane," he said, laughing, sounding as scared as he felt, as the dark runway and the car lights dropped away from them.

"You could have told me," Nicole said.

They flew on into the dark, leaving behind a nightmare, heading directly toward another one.

Chapter 13

Simnasho

Abnormal and his group made it to the turn to Simnasho later than he thought. There was a lot more booze than he had counted on, and he didn't want to leave any of it.

One mile before they got to the town of Simnasho, he rode up beside Rosebud, and signaled for him to pull over. The caravan stopped on the road in a dark high meadow.

"Get'm together, back by the trucks."

They parked their bikes and Abnormal Norman walked with the men to the vehicles. "We get back here," he told Rosebud, "take a count of how many we have." The group, which Rosebud reported to be twenty-two men and eleven women, were passing bottles around when they got back to the trucks. That was fine. Drunk and mean.

"Alright, we will go into this little town like shit through a goose. If you haven't been here before, all of the commercial buildings and most of the houses will be on the left as we come in. I want the fire hall and the longhouse intact, as well as the gas station. We keep the girls alive, kill everyone else. We will clean out the houses tonight and at first light. Don't drink so much that you can't function. Everyone armed with your favorite shooter. We're going to go in fast and hard, killing anyone who stands against us. All the vehicles, go to the fire hall. First two bikes take the store. Then we'll assemble at the fire station. Begin clearing the houses out. Questions?"

A tall thin man with tattoos on his face and arms raised his hand. Norman pointed at him.

"What is it, Razor?"

"Can I have one of the Indian girls?"

Abnormal laughed. "This ain't a catch and release world no more. You catch'm, you clean'm."

Headlights came up behind their stopped caravan, and then a horn sounded. Norman pointed at Mike and Jaz.

"Kill'm and get their car. We get to the fire station, I want all these roads blocked into and out of our town. Let' s move."

As he got on his scooter, he heard gunfire coming from behind him, and smiled. The world was now ruled by gunfire. They rode into the small town of Simnasho five minutes later.

It was over before it started. Rosebud took two others with him to the store. Norman rode up to the fire station and got off his bike. As he entered the front door, George Stands Alone came out of the dark into the office, and Norman shot him point blank in the chest with his Colt .45. George fell backwards on the floor and didn't move.

"Clear this place out," he told Mike, "and get rid of the rest of the Indians. This is my headquarters. I'm the warden." He laughed, and said, "And get rid of this dead one."

Shots and screams came from the longhouse, and Norman knew he had made the right decision. This was his new jail, and he was the warden.

Chapter 14

Simnasho

Martha hadn't thought about it much, but if she did, she never knew she would live this long. She had seen many things in her eighty-six years. She grew up with parents who accepted life and taught her the old ways, ways she now knew would be invaluable. It was not her time now, of that she was certain. The Siyapu doctor at the clinic had told her to slow down some, and wanted her to take the little white pills for her heart. But her heart was just fine, it was the way of things. She did take the little aspirin as he had told her. Aspirin after all, came from the bark of the tree.

She drew back from the door and pulled Gopher with her. Motorcycles and gunshots and screams came up the driveway from the town, a football field distance away.

She had been waiting for this since the first gunshots at the store.

She had hurried out to the barn with Gopher, he holding the lantern, as she saddled the mare, and then put a halter on her cow. They left them in the barn and went back to the house. She placed two canvas bags on the kitchen table, and put candles, jerky, roots, dried berries, a water bag in one and a canteen in the other.

"Gopher, bring the lantern to the bedroom." He followed her, and she went ahead, as much from decades of finding her way in the dark as by the flickering light of the lantern. From the closet she pulled out a large canvas scabbard and lugged it past Gopher to the kitchen. She took the leather thongs off and pulled out her husband's lever action Winchester 44-40 rifle. The same caliber as the handgun. Two boxes of shells went into each canvas bag. She loaded the rifle and put it back in the scabbard, and placed in into one of the duffle bags. She sat in a chair and felt a weariness come over her that she hadn't felt in a long time. But there was work to do, and it was up to her to do it. She had much to teach kids like her grandson.

When the motorcycle noise roared by on the road below, she told Gopher, "blow out the light!"

They walked carefully through the dark living room and looked out. There were headlights down at the Fire and Safety building, and others at the store. Gunshots and screams.

"*Ala*, what should we do?" Gopher whispered.

"We have to leave, soon." They stood there and looked for a moment longer, and watched as a figure ran from the Fire and Safety building down the road, followed by two larger figures. Men. The figure darted away from them, and then ran headlong up Martha's gravel driveway.

"Gopher, get me my gun, the revolver."

"*Ala*!"

"Do it now. Hurry."

Martha opened her front door slightly, and waited. The first runner was small, and was getting some distance from the two, who Martha was sure were men from the motorcycles.

When the figure was just twenty feet away, almost to Gopher's car, Martha opened the door, the house dark behind her, and said quietly, "Here, come here."

The small figure slowed, and then ran straight for the door. Martha opened the door all the way, and Gopher touched her arm with the 44-40 Colt revolver. Martha grabbed the heavy gun with her right hand, and Cecilia Wanamaker ran headlong into her.

Martha staggered back under the girl's weight, and said sharply, "Gopher, take her."

"The men," she cried, "They killed George, and chased me, they're right . . ."

The first one came around the car and flashed a light right at Martha. "C'mere, little chicken," he said, and came toward the door, and Martha pulled the revolver up with both hands and shot him in the middle of the chest, the gun bucking up and she let it drop down, swinging it toward the other man who had run up beside his partner, almost to the door now, and Martha shot him in the face, his head exploding as he ran forward, his lifeless body dropping at her feet. As he fell, he looked like a pig she had once shot. She had blessed the pig, for it was provided by the Creator for their nourishment.

This man was from the Devil, and she had grieved more for the pig. She had to move her feet back as he fell, the arthritis sending a jolt of pain up her legs. She had too much to do to make these *miyanas* (children) safe.

"Jesus Christ!" Gopher said, his arms around Cecilia, a sixteen-year-old tribal girl who had grown up around him and his cousins and family.

Martha closed the door and stood, breathing heavy, her heart thudding in her narrow chest.

"Jesus, *Ala*, you killed those men!"

"Yes, and there will be more coming. We must hurry." She turned and pulled Gopher and Cecilia to her. "We have no time for thinking about this, we have to leave. There will be other killings here tonight, and the Lord has given you children to me to get to the Agency." She touched Cecilia's face in the dark. "Child, you okay to travel?"

She felt Cecilia's nod.

"Gopher, you and Cece each take a bag. I'll carry the lantern and we'll make our way to the barn in the dark."

In the barn Martha risked lighting the lantern. She had to show the children how to put the bags on each side of the saddle. She blew out the light and opened the side door, not looking at the town where there were still gunshots and yelling.

"*Ala*, the cow, she isn't moving."

Martha moved back and tried, and in the end, she left the door open for a way for the cow to get out. Her cow was probably going to be hamburger by the end of the week, but they didn't have time to try to take her with them now.

Her mare was skittish, and Martha talked to her as she led her through the pasture to the tree line up above her house. Off to her right, two blocks up from the longhouse, a residence flared up in fire, the Gun Shows house, she was certain, but she was not an army, and knew that to go back to try to help would mean the death of all of them.

She found the path in the trees, and set off on a walk in the dark, going by her senses as much as anything. It was pitch dark in the woods.

Her mare was still spooky. The gunshots and the fires had the horse on the edge of bolting. Martha talked softly to her horse.

She reached into her bag and pulled out a small flashlight. "Gopher, Cece, I'm going to give you this flashlight. You two walk just ahead of me, let the horse see the trail. If I tell you to turn the light out, do it right away."

They walked like that for a mile, Martha reckoned, and the route took them back around the Graber's house and back to Hwy 3, out of sight of the town. They came out of the woods and stood there, looking at the dark highway below them.

With the light off, Martha led them down into the meadow, and quickly across the highway. *Might as well be now as later*, she thought, *before the bad men started widening their search for In-dins*. Across the highway they walked along the meadow, and into the trees on the far side. There were no more roads to cross for the next twenty miles, and if she could get them over the next ridge, they could spend the night without the bad men from town (as she thought of them) finding them. And if the bad men did find them, she would not hesitate to use the old guns her husband had kept oiled, and taught her to keep away from the politicians.

Martha followed Gopher and Cece down the trail, her feet finding the place to step. She couldn't see where she was walking, Gopher held the light down, lighting the way up in front. Martha held on to the mare, and was able to follow the light ahead. The trees were close around them for a time, and now they were in the high meadow, south of the road, and over the ridge. When they got to the meadow, the moonlight was enough for them to see, and she told Gopher to turn the flashlight off. She knew the bad men would not follow them. The Siyapu would not be able to track them, and they had other things to do, like kill her people.

Martha knew they needed to stop, and would have to soon. The moonlight made stark black shadows where the spirits, the stick people, danced.

Martha Couer d' Alenes hurt. Her hands were swollen with the arthritis, and her knees and feet weren't any better. That old arthritis was a bad one to get ate up with, she knew and she had it in what felt like every joint. She didn't want the young ones to see, but maybe they should see what it was to be an elder. Old age was not for *kiyaak* (the weak).

I don't know how I was able to use Georges' old gun to shoot those bad Siyapu, but I did, and they deserved it. I just have so much pain in my hands.

Martha knew at some level that the shooting of the men was not a bad thing, and she didn't hold the thought the youngsters had about life. She would have just as soon stepped on a spider, a bug in the house. They were vermin.

But my hands, how did I do that? I am pulling my horse, but I am ready to lay down. No, you can't yet until you tell the kids how things work, how to sleep, to make it in the woods.

Fire first, and I can get it going and use it to guide the others from Simnasho, her friends. Then we find food.

Her grandson walked ahead on the faint trail in the meadow.

"Gopher, in those trees just ahead, let's stop."

"Okay, *Ala*." He said something to Cecilia, and they set off, with Martha moving the horse. Her heart smiled at what she saw. She knew that they were in for a lot of death, that many tribal members and others would die, but Indian leaders were made during times of great adversity. Gopher was looking out for his *Ala*, and now for Cecilia. He was a boy in the morning, and now overnight, her grandson had become a man. As it should be.

"Is this good, *Ala*?"

She looked around. They were in the trees, but could still see the meadow. Anyone coming on their back trail would be highlighted in the meadow with the moonlight.

"This is perfect, Grandson. Help me with the packs." She led the horse into a small clearing, and tied the rope to a branch. Gopher and Cecilia came up and untied the packs. When they placed the first one on the ground, Martha sat heavily down on it, her bones on fire. Gopher came over, a worried look on his face.

"*Ala*, let me help you make a blanket." She nodded, smiling to herself.

"Grandson, you are now a man." She saw a look pass between Gopher and Cecilia. The girl smiled.

"Can I get you some water, some jerky?" Cece asked Martha.

"Thank you dear, that would be nice, I just need to rest for a minute."

Gopher and the girl made a little camp, and Gopher used the flashlight to spread out the blankets. He placed rocks against a tree, away from the meadow, and set about starting a small fire, using a lighter and a candle. Cecilia gathered twigs and dried branches. He soon had a small fire going, and helped his *Ala* with her bag for a chair over closer to the fire.

He and Cece walked up to a rise and built a fire to signal the others. They had decided that the bad men would not walk into the woods on this night. Those running from Simnasho could see it. Eleven of them came in the night. They got the fire going and walked back down to their camp.

"*Ala*."

She looked up.

"*Ala*, tomorrow, you will ride the mare, we'll situate the bags, maybe even carry one."

"I am fine, Gopher."

"*Ala*, for this once, please do as I ask. We need you here, and at the Agency. With you riding, we may be able to make it tomorrow night. Please say yes."

She nodded. It would be good to ride.

Martha looked on as Gopher spread her blanket closest to the fire, then Cecilia's, and then his. He was now the protector.

Here comes Gopher with my bag. I almost said something when he reached in and brought out the revolver. It shined in the firelight, and then he handed it to me. I checked the loads and placed it on my blanket. And now what's this? My grandson, the new man, is asking for me to teach him how to use it. Tomorrow on our trip, he said. Tomorrow. And I'm tired, and need to sleep.

And now he's showing Cecilia how to tie the horse to the tree, and then tie a rope to his wrist. The horse will act as a watchdog, sensing anything approaching, and her nervousness will wake him.

I didn't know he even would remember the lessons as a child. We're going to have to teach all of them the old ways to survive.

Tomorrow, I will teach this new man how to shoot. And the girl too.

What's Gopher doing? He is pulling a rock from the around the fire, and wrapping it in an old shirt. He put the shirt-covered rock at the foot of my blanket. Yes, he is a new man.

Gopher and Cece sat together. She leaning against him and they listened as Martha sang a prayer in Sahaptin, a song of thanks.

Thank you, God, for bringing me my grandson, and a fine man he is becoming. If there is anything good to come of this, it is to see him as a man, and he may already have his woman picked out for him. Thank you, Lord, for bringing us here. And my, does that warm rock feel good.

And after a day of losing electricity, a day of killing, a day of running – Martha Couer d'Alenes, a tribal member, an elder of the Confederated Tribes of the Cold River Indians of Oregon, fell asleep.

Chapter 15

Oregon/California border

Weasel and Nicole flew on through the night, and sometime before dawn, Weasel figured they were crossing the border with Oregon. He looked over at Nicole, and saw that she was nodding. They had talked for the first couple of hours, watching the darkened land below, pointing at occasional fires and explosions on the ground. At one point south of Sacramento they saw a huge explosion and fire, a tank farm Weasel thought. The landscape and now more than frequent fires made the flight unsettling, a flight into the unknown. The constant drone of the Lycoming engine had finally lulled his passenger into a doze. Weasel had flown too many hours, been in too many cockpits to succumb to sleep. He played games to keep himself alert. He scanned the instruments, and then looked outside at the blackness. As far as private planes go, his was a new one, a Cessna 172S Skyhawk, a 2004 model. Many of the Cessna 172's produced in 1956 were still flying.

He looked over to his right and saw Nicole watching him. He nodded and smiled. She stretched and brought her hand down lightly on his shoulder.

"I don't know if I told you how much I appreciate making this journey with you. For what it's worth, thank you, Len, uh, Weasel."

"I'm glad you're here, Nicole. I mean that. I'm glad you pushed the issue, so to speak. This would have been a lonely flight into the unknown by myself."

"That's really what we're doing, right? Flying into the unknown?"

Weasel looked out at the darkness. "Yes, only because we don't know what we will find on the way. We are maybe halfway there. I've been as lean as possible, eleven thousand feet, at just over fifty percent cruise, maybe one hundred forty miles per hour, but our true ground speed is slower. I've been running over the figures in my head, and I think we will have to find gas somewhere, and that will be dangerous if we set down at the wrong place."

"What's that?" Nicole pointed ahead, to the right. About two o'clock.

That, Weasel thought, *is the flame from two jet fighters taking off. Hope they're not coming up for us.*

"Those are two fast-movers, F-111's I think, taking off from Kingsley Field, an Air Force base at Klamath Falls." They watched as the flames turned to the west as they climbed.

"They should pass behind us on that course." They watched as the planes accelerated up and out of sight, now to their left. "They are probably going to check out a bogey off the Pacific Coast, they'll be over water in minutes."

Nicole was looking at a map with a small flashlight. "Can we land there? The airbase?"

"I don't think we should try. If they don't like it, they might shoot us. They are most assuredly on a war readiness. I think we should fly on."

Nicole turned to Weasel, her face framed by the light from the instruments. She smiled.

"Whatever you think, my captain." She touched his shoulder.

"The sun will be up in an hour. Doze if you can," Weasel said. He was becoming more and more sure of his decision to have her go with him. "At the worst case of gas consumption, we can get close. I know of a lot of little air strips we can try if we can't make it. Maybe even some ranches. We'll both look in the daylight if we need to put down."

"How big is the airport on the reservation?" Nicole asked without looking up from the map. She turned to Weasel. He laughed.

"Not big at all, in fact there isn't an airport there at all."

"I thought we were going to land there."

"We'll land on a road on the reservation."

"You sure?"

"I've done it before," Weasel said. "With a large jet. This should be easy." He smiled. Easy. He would remember those words. Easy. This would prove to be deadly and dangerous, but not "easy."

They flew on in the dark, and Weasel could now see the first hint of a false dawn to the east. He thought about this woman with him, a person he had known for some time, but really didn't know much about her. She was confident in the way she approached life. He thought she was pretty, but they had never talked about personal lives. As the sky grew lighter, he decided to talk about personal stuff. They were on a journey that might prove to be fatal at any moment. He looked over at Nicole.

"We've flown together for about a year now. We talk about planes, flying – we just never talk about you."

Nicole looked ahead, and finally answered. "I wanted to learn to fly."

"Yeah, but still…."

"I'm a nurse, a surgical nurse, and have been a reserve deputy for a few years, and have, no had, a cat."

"That's a pretty short bio," Weasel said with a smile. A cat. A high pressure job with a high pressure volunteer job. Sounds like the lady is trying to fill her days and nights with things. She's never talked about another person in her life.

"Well, that's pretty much it," Nicole said, and she looked out the side window, away from Weasel.

"Hey," he said, softly, "I didn't mean to pry, just wondering."

"What?"

"You ever get lonely?" There, he said it, trying to get an opening into who this person Nicole is.

"Yes," she said after a minute. "Sometimes, sure. Nicole Kennedy has cat."

Weasel laughed, and she smiled and turned to look at him.

"There is lonely, a loneliness that's manageable, and then there is lonely, the stark loneliness you have when you are in a relationship that's gone bad."

Weasel nodded.

"Unspeakable," Nicole said in a whisper. Weasel looked ahead, started to say something, and then stopped. He wanted to hear her, to get to know her.

"Unspeakable, empty loneliness, more empty than life itself." She looked over at Weasel and gave him a wry grin.

"So, I have a cat and volunteer, I have a life with manageable loneliness. Okay, now I've said too much."

"No," Weasel said. "Thank you, Nicole Kennedy. Although I've never thought that you look like a Kennedy."

"I was born Hernandez. After my divorce six years ago from Kennedy, I just kept the name." She made a sad face for an instant. "What about you, Mr. Pilot?"

Weasel gave a sigh, and said, "I will talk about me. We have all day in this plane together."

As it turned out, they didn't have all day.

They were quiet, and Nicole leaned back and it looked as if she was sleeping. The sky grew lighter, and after a time she stretched and looked out.

"It's beautiful," she said. As the approaching sun turned the night into grey dawn, they could see the Cascade Mountain Range to their left. Weasel knew that they had passed Crater Lake National Park within the last thirty minutes, and now they were above Oregon Highway 97, with the shadows of Mt. Thielsen going from black to light.

The first rays of the morning sun hit the cabin, and Weasel reached for his sunglasses. He pointed up ahead to the mountain range. It was now full light. “That’s Diamond Peak, with Crescent Lake in front of it.”

“I have never been up here before.”

“This mountain range runs on the west side of the reservation. We have areas on the reservation that are this beautiful. More.” He looked at Nicole. “How was your nap?”

“Good, I’m sorry I nodded off.”

“Don’t be silly. You might have to fly before we get there.”

“I can’t fly your plane, I don’t think --”

Weasel hit the autopilot button and took the yoke. He had a soft touch on the controls. His feet rode the rudder pedals. “Remember, flying this plane is made easy by having the right trim. This is what I want you to do, and I’m serious, Nicole. I want you to take the yoke, and put your feet on the pedals.”

She looked at him and then did as he asked.

“Your airplane,” he said, and dropped his hands to his lap.

“Wait!” The plane dipped, and Nicole automatically corrected.

Weasel smiled. “See, you haven’t forgotten.”

“Yes, but I only have thirty hours in a fixed wing aircraft, and it was a Cessna 152, a lot smaller than this.”

“Same thing, same-o,” Weasel said, and closed his eyes.

“You can’t go to sleep, you can’t. I need your help with this thing.”

"I won't," Weasel said, "But it sure was good to close my eyes for a second. He sat up straight and looked at the gas gauge. "We are not going to make it without a little more gas. I've been going over the figures most of the night, and tried to make this as lean as I could, but we are going to be fifty to seventy-five miles short."

"What are we going to do?"

"Land soon, before the natives," and with this he gave her a smile, "before the natives are up and restless." He pointed to the map Nicole had been looking at. "Let's look at landing someplace to the northeast, on a ranch south and east of Bend. I think that's our best chance to find some gas and avoid trouble." She held up the map.

"There, north of Fort Rock, I know of a landing strip on a ranch with a hanger. There should be some gas there. We only need a few gallons to be safe. Before we commit to losing altitude, let's pick out a couple of potential sites."

They looked, and Weasel tapped the map.

"There. The Anderson Ranch. I've been there before. A hard gravel strip, used to have some fuel." And with that, he pushed the throttle in a little, the steady drone of the engine now lower, and the nose dipped.

"Trim," he told Nicole, keeping his hands in his lap.

"You should do this," her voice rising.

"You will be fine, think of a plan to lose about five hundred feet a minute. Remember, in this country, the high desert to the east, we will be landing at about four thousand feet above sea level. We're only seven thousand feet AGL (Above ground level) so it won't take us long."

"What heading."

"That's my girl," Weasel said, getting a smile, almost a grimace in return. He watched Nicole as a pilot. He liked her concentration, with a frown line between her eyes. He consulted the map. He gave her the heading.

"Start a slow turn to that heading." He watched as she began the turn, a bobble, and then gentle turn. She gave him a quick flash grin as she had the new heading, and then concentrated out the windscreen. She flicked her eyes down at the instruments, and then did a scan outside, left to right.

Good pilot, Weasel thought.

"We don't have a tower where we're going, nor does the landing strip have ATIS, as I remember."

"Where are we landing?"

"Little place called Fort Rock. Let's start the pre-landing check."

"Roger that, Weasel. Okay, uh, fuel mixture rich, switch to both tanks, both mags on, flaps, landing lights on…."

"No. No landing lights. We're not going to alert anyone if we can help it."

Nicole turned the switch off.

"There," Weasel said. "At two o'clock."

Nicole looked.

Weasel had been here two other times, taking goose hunters to the area. The airstrip was long enough, and in the past, there was gas there. *There better be some gas there, or we are in trouble.*

"I see the town," Nicole said, "And the airstrip, with the hangers, the windsock." The landscape around the airstrip was flat, with sagebrush surrounding the runway.

"Wind direction."

"None," Nicole said. The windsock was limp.

"Let's land to the south, come around on a typical downwind run." He watched as Nicole flew by the airstrip. There was no activity on the ground, but it was early, just before sunup. That didn't mean that they wouldn't draw some interest. A unincorporated community of thirteen hundred, there would be people around, and probably some of them would be up. They would have to get in and get out fast if the locals didn't want to part with gas.

Throttle down, they would come in quiet.

"Why don't you land your plane?" Nicole said, risking a glance at Weasel.

"No. I'll be with you and will guide you through it, but you don't need me. Just do what you have trained to do. You may have to land without me at some point."

Weasel didn't know how soon that would be.

They came in over the sagebrush, past a ranch, and Nicole lined up on the mile-long paved runway, out in the middle of the high desert.

"We're in the middle of the fucking desert," Nicole said, looking ahead at the small town, just out of the trees.

"Keep it high, land down toward the other end, we can stop a lot quicker than you think, I don't want to taxi very long, give them a chance to see us."

Nicole concentrated, the sun just coming up to her left, her eyes checking. Weasel was the consummate instructor, watching, letting her build her confidence in the plane. They came over the numbers at two hundred feet. Perfect. The runway was a mile long. There was a house to the left, and as they got half way down the runway, a cluster of hangers. The town was up ahead and to the right. A Chevron station sign.

No sign of anyone, maybe all sleeping. Maybe they didn't know what happened in the world? The power must go out here often.

As they approached the middle hanger, Weasel pointed down, and Nicole flared the plane. With a slight bounce, they were on the ground and started to roll out, the engine at an idle. It was possible, Weasel thought, that no one saw or heard them, the engine was throttled back as they began their approach.

Nicole threw him a glance, and smiled, now a big grin.

"I did it!" She said, the excitement in her voice made Weasel smile, as tired as he was. Weasel pointed ahead. On the right, there was an office and hanger, and that was where he wanted to be.

"Let's just stop in front. Stay in your seat, and shut the engine down. I'm going to get out and turn the plane around in case we have to leave fast."

"K."

Weasel got out and went to the tail and began to turn the plane. Nicole helped by turning the nose wheel to the right, so he could swing the plane around.

Cold. It was colder than he thought, but it was spring in the high desert, and he was used to L.A.

Shit, it must be thirty degrees. He looked around, and didn't see any movement. The town was quiet. He got the plane turned around and pointed back down the runway. He looked up at Nicole and grinned and motioned for her to get out. She jumped down and threw her arms around him and gave him a hug.

Weasel pointed at her bag. "Get your Glock, we might need it."

She nodded, and put her Glock on her hip. They started off for the office.

"Damn," Nicole said, rubbing her arms. "This isn't L.A."

Weasel smiled. They approached the office in the corner of the hanger closest to the town. He was hoping that the electricity outage hadn't created too much of a problem this far out in the middle of Bum Fuck Egypt, as they used to say as kids, but he knew they couldn't count on it. He wanted to buy some gas; that was his first choice.

He glanced back at his plane, and then walked up to the office door. As he got closer, he saw that the jam was smashed, and slightly open. He pointed at it as Nicole came up beside him.

"Someone's already been here. Keep your gun ready." He pushed the door open and stepped inside, Nicole following close behind.

There were logbooks and papers strewn on the floor, a chair tipped over behind the desk. Weasel stepped around the chair and entered a hallway and stopped. There was a body on the floor, halfway down the hallway.

"Nicole!" He pointed at the body as she looked around him.

She stepped around Weasel, her gun out and ready, and bent to examine the body.

"Dead," she said. "He's been shot." And indeed he had, Weasel saw. A gunshot wound to the forehead meant that this person wouldn't be flying anywhere anytime soon. A man of about forty, with graying hair, wearing blue coveralls.

Weasel looked around. "I wanted to buy some gas, but now we get some and get the hell out of here. Stay close. I will try to find gas and refuel. You just stay alert."

He found two gas cans in the second hanger and opened the filler cap of one and looked. It looked and smelled like JP100, the fuel they needed. Couldn't do anything about it now if it wasn't. He found a funnel on a bench and handed it to Nicole and picked up the cans, grunting with the weight.

Weasel walked outside with the cans, Nicole following. Their Cessna (and now he thought of it as theirs) looked forlorn on the runway, fifty yards away, like an obedient pet waiting for its owner. The sun was now full up to their left, a round orb coming up from the high desert floor, the sagebrush orange.

They started for the plane and stopped suddenly when a series of gunshots came from over by the Chevron station. He walked faster. He got to the plane and set the cans down, looking toward the town. Still quiet except for the gunshots of a minute ago.

"I'm going up on the refueling step. Hand me a can when I get up." Nicole holstered her Glock and picked up a can, her face a grimace. "You should see you," Weasel said with a laugh. She struggled with both hands to hold the can up, and Weasel reached down and pulled it up. Not the balancing act. He actually got most of the gas in, and exchanged cans, with a nervous Nicole pacing beside the plane. As he poured the last of the five gallon can, Nicole spoke, her voice low, urgent.

"Weasel!"

He looked down at her and she pointed. "Some men at the office, going inside."

He stepped down and moved the cans away from the plane.

"Gun out and behind me."

They came around the plane and Weasel waved at the man outside, watching them.

"They shot Jim." The voice yelled from inside the office. Two more men came out, three altogether, two in their twenties, the speaker a large man of about fifty, with a grey beard. He carried a handgun down by his side, glaring at Weasel and Nicole.

"He was dead when we got here," Weasel said.

Nicole spoke up. "I'm a nurse, he's been dead most of the night. We want to pay for the gas." She pointed at the office. "We didn't do that."

The large man came closer. "Doesn't matter what the fuck you did, your plane stays until we sort this out."

"I'm a deputy as well," Nicole said, moving out from behind Weasel. He loved her then for her nerve, her ability to take charge, when most wouldn't. It happened fast then.

The bearded man brought the gun up and at the same time Nicole pulled her Glock, and the bearded man shot Weasel from twenty feet, and Nicole shot him with a two handed grip, Weasel noticing the Glock jumping in her hand, the bullets hitting the man in the chest, the man falling, and Weasel yelling "Ow," and he fell, heavy on his side. A sledgehammer hit his arm, a thousand bees, a knife. He had those thoughts all at once as blood spurted from his arm. He dimly heard Nicole tell the others to run, or she would shoot them.

She appeared above him and grabbed his arm. It felt like someone had punched his left upper arm, just below his shoulder, and blood was pouring down. "Ow, shit!"

Nicole sat him up and then pulled.

Oh God, ohmigod, what the hell just happened, you just killed a man. No time for that now, think, focus, Nicole. You're a nurse.

"Weasel, we have to go, help me, stand up!" They struggled and he stood, swaying on her, leaning against her. She reached up and opened the right door to the plane, and pushed Weasel in and shut the door. She ran around and got into the left seat. She grabbed Weasel's right arm and put his hand over the wound.

"Hold that tight to stop the bleeding, we are going." She hit the ignition and the prop spun and the engine came to life. She pushed in the throttle part way and the plane moved forward. She wasn't planning to take off just yet, but wanted to move down the runway away from the buildings. They only needed a small part of the runway to take off.

"Weasel, talk to me, help me, talk me into a take-off sequence."

He told her. Flaps, trim. carb heat. She didn't wait for more, and pushed the throttle all the way in, and when they had more than enough speed for rotation, she pulled back on the yoke and the Cessna jumped into the air. She was too busy to worry about Weasel now, but leveled off at 1500 with a heading roughly NW and turned her attention to him. She needed him now.

"Weasel, look at me." Nicole kept her left hand on the yoke, and with her right hand she reached behind her and rummaged in her pack. She felt a roll of vet wrap and pulled it to her lap. This wasn't going to be pretty, but she had to stop the bleeding. She pulled the cellophane off with her teeth, and unrolled a section of the spongy, sticky wrap.

"Weasel, lean forward." She gently motioned him to a more upright position, and as easy as she could, she started to unroll the vet wrap on the wound. She knew that it would hurt like hell, but there were no other options. She leaned over and looked at Weasel, and he gave her a weak smile.

"Stupid of me to get in the way of that bullet," he said, and started to laugh, and then stopped with an "Ow." He looked at Nicole and smiled. "You are quite the warrior, woman."

"Weasel, with your right hand, can you fly for a minute."

He nodded.

She moved his left arm up, gently, and began wrapping the vet wrap around the wound. Weasel grimaced and tried to move away, but she finally got the job done. "It should stop most of the bleeding. How long to the reservation?"

"Less than an hour."

"Uh," he said, "I think I'm going to be sick." And with that, he retched, and then threw up in his lap, the smell acrid in the plane. Nicole reached behind her and found a shirt in her bag.

"Here, use this to wipe it off."

"I'm sorry," he said, a flush going to his face. He fumbled with the shirt, letting his left arm rest on the trim control.

"Sorry," he muttered again.

"I'm a nurse, remember. I want you to hang on, I'm going to get us there. You stay with me so you can help me land. Oh, what heading for the reservation?"

Weasel gave her the heading. "We should be coming in east of Bend, and then Redmond, just east of the Redmond airport. You will see it in a bit."

Nicole opened her vent, the smell of the vomit sharp in the cabin. She was worried about Weasel. He was going into shock, and she needed him to get them there.

I think I can land this thing, no, you know you can, Nicole. Remember your lessons, your solo flight. Just keep it together.

As a nurse, if often helped to talk to herself, and now she needed to talk to Weasel, to keep him in the game.

"I'm staying about 1500 AGL, Weasel, what do you think?" The land to the east and ahead was high desert – sagebrush, Juniper trees, and rock formations. To the west and ahead was national forest.

"Uh, okay, whatever you think." Weasel sounded sleepy, not good.

"Stay with me, Weasel. Okay, I see a larger city over to the left, about ten o'clock."

"Bend. Area of about one hundred fifty thousand."

"How far now?"

"Twenty minutes. I'm going to nap for a minute."

"No! Weasel, what is that?" She wanted to keep him engaged, needed him to be in the game. Once they were down, she would take care of him. She pointed ahead, and to her left.

"Redmond airport. A two mile runway. Don't go there."

Nicole flew on, looking, her hands wet, her heart beating. Weasel was nodding.

"Weasel!" She yelled, and his head came up sharply. "Weasel, we should be close, just passed Madras airport." She knew from the map that Madras was but ten miles from the reservation. The land suddenly fell away, a lake of some sort to her left, and steep river canyon just ahead.

"Uh, fly the canyon, and as soon as we cross the river, start your landing procedure. Anywhere on the road, the highway on the reservation." His words were slurred, and he slumped against the shoulder harness.

Shit. Now what? Okay, land the fucking plane, Nicole.

She flew the river at the height of the surrounding land, and then she saw the bridge, and left the river, flying north.

Flaps. Carb heat. Power down. Line up on the road. She flew past a lumber mill, then the museum and casino. Shit, still too high. She pulled back on the power a little more. Still too high. She glanced over at Weasel, and back at the road. Lower. Power off. She flared the plane, going as slow as she dared, her right hand on the throttle in case she had to go around, but she knew that this was it, there was no way she wanted to line up again for a landing.

Shell station on her left. One car coming from the hill, and it suddenly veered off, as if the driver had seen the plane.

The wheels hit, bounced, and then they were down, and Nicole kept the Cessna on the center line, and started to apply the brakes. She came to an intersection, and brought the plane to a stop. She looked over at Weasel as she turned the engine off. It was quiet in the plane.

"Weasel, can you hear me?" She felt his pulse on his carotid, and it was fast, thread. Shit. A knock on her door startled her, and she looked over to see the face of a tribal police officer, a large Indian with long black hair. She opened the door.

"Why you landing on the Rez?" he asked, not friendly. She pointed. "Weasel. He needs help, he's been shot." The face immediately changed, a smile, and he looked around Nicole to look at Weasel. He spoke urgently into his radio, calling for an ambulance. After that, things happened fast.

"Take care of the plane, I'm going with him," Nicole said as she got out and went around to Weasel's door. The officer followed her.

"Who are you?" He asked.

"I'm the one who got him and his plane here. Help me with him."

She got into the ambulance after they loaded him, and took one look at the plane. She leaned over Weasel as they rode in the rocking ambulance, medics working to get Weasel stable. He opened his eyes and looked around.

"Plane?" he croaked, his gaze coming to Nicole.

She nodded. "Weasel, we're on the reservation."

"Did we crash?" He looked around, his eyes darting in a wild swing.

"No, silly. Captain in charge Nicole landed the plane," she said, and then added, "Weasel, you're home."

Simnasho
Fire and Safety Building

Abnormal leaned back in the former fire chief's chair and took a long pull on a bottle of Johnny Walker Blue. All in all it hadn't gone too bad, except for the two idiots who got killed at some Indian's house, chasing a girl in the dark. He had slept in the chair, and took a drink as soon as his eyes opened.

Mike and Jaz lounged in chairs on the other side of the office.

"You want a young'n?" Mike asked. "We got some of the people, and a few young locked up over there in the big building."

Abnormal leaned forward and laughed. "It's called a 'longhouse' you uncouth heathen, and yeah, I want a young'n. Might as well see what we have here." He took another drink and waited for his reward for taking over this shithole.

Chapter 16

Cold River Tribal Police Administration

Martin opened his eyes and felt as if he had consumed a quart of tequila. He had always thought that that shit should be a controlled substance, even the smooth stuff. His mouth tasted as if a thousand turkeys had camped there, as the saying goes. He leaned forward, rocking his office chair to an upright position. His neck hurt. He had slept maybe an hour and a half. The shades were drawn in his office. Lori was sitting in a chair with her head cradled on her arms on his conference table over in the corner. Below her on the floor – Jennifer with her head on a pillow, Laurel curled up beside her. Smokey was nowhere around.

The meeting had gone on until just before dawn, with one emergency after another, officers running all over the reservation to quell shootings, stop looting, and keep the people on the highway from killing each other. They had made the decision to close the road from Portland at the northern boundary, on a case by case basis. The traffic had slowed to a trickle anyway, and they had reports of cars being shot up as they approached Government Camp, on the Mt. Hood pass. Highway 26 was blocked in several places before people had a chance to make the reservation.

Stay home, that's what he would tell people.

He stretched, and slowly stood up. He moved carefully around to his desk and opened a small refrigerator and removed a bottle of water. As he turned he saw Lori watching him, her eyes open, not moving. He smiled.

She slowly sat up and smiled back, stretched, stood and walked over and kissed him.

"Let me rinse my mouth," Martin said, and added, "Yuck."

"Come here, husband, I'll kiss you any old way and time."

As she leaned into him and they kissed, his office door opened and Smokey stuck his head in.

Had he slept? Martin wondered.

Smokey motioned with his head for Martin. He looked at his wife and daughter on the floor and nodded at them, smiling.

Martin and Lori joined Smokey in the administration section. They took chairs, the secretaries and receptionist gone.

"Boss, we need to do something with the jail. We have forty-nine prisoners, most misdemeanants, a few felons, and a handful of inmates waiting for transport to federal lockup in Portland."

"What do you think?"

"Bluefeathers said for us to do what we needed, including letting them all go."

"All of them?" Martin had thought about it, but there were a couple of murderous bastards in there. He looked at Lori. She shrugged her shoulders, yawned, and stood up.

"I'm going to find some coffee, some food and water for Jennifer and Laurel and me. You boys carry on." She leaned over and gave Martin a kiss, winked at Smokey, and walked back into Martin's office. Smokey grinned.

When they entered the jail, the noise was overwhelming. Inmates were banging on the bars up and down the corridors. A frustrated correctional officer met them in the day room.

"Where is everyone?" Martin asked.

Gloria Running Horse looked as if she hadn't slept at all. Thirty, short, with long black hair, she wore glasses and always appeared near-sighted. Martin knew she was a hard worker.

"I'm it, Chief."

"Damn," Martin said. "Let's get the inmates in "A" dorm out first, the ones with short time left." Smokey went with Gloria, and when they stepped in the corridor, the noise increased. He could hear Smokey shouting over the noise, and it quieted somewhat. Smokey led a dozen men, all tribal members, out into the day room and ordered them to sit.

"Most of you have heard that the electricity is out." A murmur rose up from the group. "As far as we know, the electricity is out over most of the United States. We don't know why, and we may never know."

"Fucking towel heads," a young Indian man from the table in the corner said, and he added," Sorry, Chief."

"We don't know why, but we must be prepared for the worst. All of you in the room are tribal members. I am letting you go, giving you an early release, on one condition."

"What's that?" a voice from the near table. Ramone Eagle.

"That you go to your families and don't commit new crimes. I want all of you to swear to that. If you are caught committing a crime after you leave here, justice will be swift, and administered by any tribal member or the police department. Any questions?"

"Can I get my stuff?"

Martin looked at Gloria. She nodded, tentative. "Our records are computerized, but I can figure out how to find their street clothes."

"Good," Martin said. "Also," he held up his hand – "When you go with Officer Running Horse you will be orderly, or we will put your sorry ass back into the jail and deal with you later. Much later. Understood?"

A chorus of nods, "Yup" and "Yeah," came back to Martin as the group filed out.

They went like that until there were four left. The inmates were not hardened, tough guys, they were gang-bangers who thought they were tough.

Murray was the first. "I don't see why you couldn't have let me go with the other group." He slumped back in his chair, a long single braid down his back. "That guy in the NFL, that quarterback, he fought dogs like me, and he went back and played football. No harm, no foul."

Smokey leaned forward. "You play football," he asked Bug.

"Nope. I just play videos mostly."

"When you can throw a football like Michael Vick we'll ask you. Otherwise, just keep going. "

Martin waited as Gloria led the last inmate into the day room. George Wolfhead. He motioned for Wolfhead to sit. Wolfhead stood and glared at Martin.

"He said sit!" Smokey barked.

Wolfhead looked at Smokey, and then took a seat across from Martin.

"I just have a few things to say," Martin said. "Keep away from NGT. We'll let you out with a promise to be a good citizen. If you are a problem, we'll put you in a cell, George, and give you food and water when we get to it, maybe once a day. The ACLU attorneys are probably figuring out how to keep from being killed by the very scumbags they put back on the street. They won't be coming 'round the bad ol' reservation anytime soon."

George looked at Martin, and then nodded.

"If you go back to jail, and the three of us here are killed, you are going to have a tough end of life."

Smokey was standing by the wall, his arms crossed, looking on.

"You good with all of this, Lieutenant Smoke?" George smiled as he said it.

"Only the part about giving you food and water. I won't bother if you come back here. I won't babysit you."

"Be a leader," Martin said. "If you and your people create a major problem, and the electricity stays off, we might just shoot you. Understood?"

George Wolfhead gave Martin a slow nod, glared at Smokey, and was led away by Gloria.

Smokey came off the wall and walked over to Martin.

"I've got some of the elders coming in here to empty out the freezers. They will dry the food the traditional Indian way, and we'll store it here in the jail, so no one can get at it until we need to dole it out."

"Good thinking," Martin said. He knew how valuable Smokey was, and would continue to be. As long as they stayed alive. Not all of them did.

Stay alive.

As they were leaving the jail to go back to the tribal police administration area, an excited Lori met them at the door.

"Chief, Smokey, you guys are not going to believe this!" She grabbed Martin's hand and pulled him toward the front door.

"What's going on wife of mine?" He was tired, and had to work to find the last of his patience.

"Husband. Come with me." She winked at Smokey, and he gave her a little smile. Martin let himself be pulled toward the door. He saw the wink she gave Smokey, and that made him relax. Some things didn't change. The McGruff girl was alive and well, and up to something.

"It's Weasel. He's here!"

Chapter 17

Indian Health Services Clinic (IHS)

Nicole sat on a bench outside the operating room in the Indian Health Services clinic. People moved around her as if she was invisible, and in a way, she was. She was weary to the core, and would have been able to sleep if it were not for the fact that a man she had bonded with was fighting for his life just a few feet away.

When Weasel had been wheeled into the clinic, she held his hand and talked with him, even as he was slipping deeper into unconsciousness. As they got into the room, a tall doctor, Semington his name plate said, had pointed at her and ordered her out.

“I’m a nurse,” she said, “and I’m not leaving.”

He pointed to the door, and then his look softened.

“If you’re a nurse, stay outside, we’re going to need you. Now let me fix Weasel.”

Nicole put her face in her hands and then looked up, sensing people close to her. A young Indian woman, very pretty and about halfway through term to pregnancy, Nicole thought, was looking down at her. She reached out and touched Nicole on the shoulder.

“I’m Lori,” she said. “You look like you had a rough trip.” Nicole noticed the blood on her hands and sleeves, holding them up and really seeing it for the first time. “Weasel’s blood,” she said.

Lori straightened and pointed to a man behind her. “This it Martin Andrews, the chief of police, the man, my man,” and then she laughed, “the man responsible for this.” She rubbed her stomach. Martin held out his hand and took Nicole’s hand. He had short salt and pepper hair. She would have made him as a cop.

“I’m glad the two of you got here,” he said.

Nicole nodded. “The plane?”

“Taken care of,” Martin said. “Under cover and under guard. I think we’re going to need it soon.” He pointed to a tall Indian man wearing a tribal police uniform. “This is Lieutenant Smokey Kukup. He is going to run security for the reservation.”

Smokey nodded at Nicole.

Lori sat down and put her arm around Nicole.

I don’t even know this woman, but I feel good with her. Nicole smiled. Lori was saying something.

“Let’s get you washed up. These two boys have to be in control. They are going to want to hear your story.” Nicole smiled, and let Lori help her up and lead her to a bathroom.

She looked in the mirror, and said, “Oh God.

Lori laughed. “Been there, living out here and all.”

Nicole rolled up her sleeves and washed her hands and face, getting most of the blood off. She tried a little smile in the mirror, and Lori put her arm around her and made a face in the mirror. “Beautiful,” she said. “Your man there in the emergency room is gonna like that, I think.”

“He’s not my man, Weasel is . . . “

"Yeah right," Lori said with a laugh. "I know these things. If he's not now, he will be. That Weasel, he needs a good woman."

They went out and Nicole sat on the Bench. Martin and Smokey were engaged in conversation with two officers. They came over when Nicole and Lori sat down.

"Nicole, tell us how you got here, how Weasel got shot." Lori said. Martin and Smokey stood close.

"Well, uh, I was a student pilot and Len, Weasel, was my instructor. We were above North L.A., in a little Robinson helicopter, and then the lights went out. Weasel, and I didn't know that was his name until later, he flew the 'copter to a private airport where he had his plane. I convinced him that I couldn't make it to my hospital." She looked up and saw that they were all listening, and began again. "I'm a nurse, and live alone. I asked Weasel to take me with him, so we flew out in the dark. Headed north. There were gunshots and fires already in the area, and along the way we could see fires.

"At daylight, Weasel said that we couldn't make it to the reservation without more gas, so we, well, I landed at a place called Fort Rock. We were going to buy gas, but the man in the station was shot dead, and we just took some.

"As Weasel finished loading the gas, three men came up and one of them shot Weasel. And I, I just, I ahh . . . shot him, three times in the chest, and I uh . . . :"

Nicole put her face in her hands and felt the tears come, rolling through her fingers and dropping on the floor. She felt Lori's arm tighten around her, the Indian woman's face on her arm. Nicole sobbed for a minute, and then she took a deep breath, and it was over. She looked up as Lori wiped her face with a towel.

"Sorry," she said, her voice shaky.

"It's okay," Lori whispered, and stroked her cheek.

"I have a question," Smokey said.

Nicole nodded.

"You said you shot him. How does it happen that you had a gun?"

"As well as being a nurse, I'm a reserve deputy for Ventura County. Weasel asked me to get my gun and put it on when we got to his hanger." She pulled her shirt up to reveal a Glock on her belt. "When we saw the dead man, Weasel said to cover him while he put the gas in. After Weasel got shot, I shoved him into the plane and took off to the north. When we were in the air I tried to stop the bleeding as best as I could. I managed to keep him awake long enough to get me on the right heading for the reservation, and I'm just so . . . so worried that I . . ."

She started crying again, just when she thought she was done. She jerked her head up after seconds, and looked from Lori to Martin to Smokey.

"Weasel said that I should come with him, but I don't even know if I can stay here."

"Of course you can," Lori said. "You're with Weasel, and that's good enough for us." She gave Martin a challenging look.

"Yes," Martin said, "and we are going to get you a uniform. We need all the help we can get."

Nicole stood up, shaky. "I'm not leaving Weasel."

"How about we do this," Martin said. "I know you just got here, but we are in serious trouble, and we can use your skills as a nurse and a cop. I'll have Lori get you a uniform and you stay here, close to Weasel, and we can use you as a guard for the Indian Health Service here. It will allow me to use the officer here for other duty."

Nicole nodded, and sat back down. Lori waved them away, saying something that sounded to Nicole like, "husband."

After a while, she let Lori convince her that Weasel wouldn't be out of surgery for some time. In the next thirty minutes, Lori took her to the tribal police department, got her a snack and a wash cloth. They laughed in the uniform room like little girls when Nicole tried on uniforms. She kept her own gun, got a duty belt, and a radio.

"Don't know how long we can charge the batteries in these," Lori said. "May have to use smoke signals," and with that, they both broke out laughing and walked up the stairs. They ran into Jennifer and Laurel as they headed for the chief's office.

Nicole laughed as they were introduced, feeling better than she thought she ever would. She looked at Jennifer's stomach.

"What is it, an epidemic around here, you both being pregnant?"

Lori gave Nicole a ride back to the clinic. "We might all be walking soon, but for now, we can drive. After the gas runs out, we will be walking to police calls, or riding horses."

Nicole waited on the bench outside the operating room, getting a few curious stares. A young woman with long black hair, wearing jeans and a sweatshirt that said Oregon Ducks, came up and sat beside her.

"I'm Jeannie," she said with a smile. "You must be the pilot, Weasel's woman."

Nicole started to tell her that she was not Weasel's woman, and then thought, *What the hell,* and just nodded.

"Nicole. And how did you know about . . . ?"

"Oh, everybody on the reservation knows by now. And you're a cop already, huh?"

"I was a cop in California . . . and a nurse."

"Well, welcome." And with that Jeannie got up and walked back to an office, chatting to people as she went, telling them about the cop, the pilot, and the nurse. Weasel's woman.

Nicole looked up as Doctor Semington came out of the OR. He raised his eyebrows at Nicole's uniform, but didn't say anything.

"Weasel should be okay," he said, the weariness showing in his face, his speech. "Lucky you got him here when you did, he was getting very shocky, and we still have some meds to get him through this. A month from now, who knows."

Nicole felt like crying again, and had a sudden thought that she had cried more today than at any time since she had been a teenager. "Thank you, Doctor. Can I see him?"

"He's out, but yes, you can go in. A nurse where?"

"Santa Barbara, surgery, all kinds. And a reserve deputy."

"And a pilot." The doctor said. His voice had softened.

How the hell do they know this stuff. I've only been here two hours.

"Just so you know, Doc," Nicole said as she walked to the door, "I'm not leaving Weasel, I'm not leaving here until he's stable."

She went in and heard the doctor mutter behind her, "A nurse, a pilot, a cop, and now you're Weasel's woman."

Weasel had the familiar IV's attached, a heart monitor, and he was out, his eyelids fluttering. Nicole touched his face and sat next to the bed. When she leaned back in the chair, her own eyes closed, and she started to doze. She dreamed instantly, a dark dream that replayed the shooting, only this time, the man with the gun in Fort Rock kept getting up and coming at them, and each time she shot him again.

A loud scream from the hallway brought her full awake. She shook her head, looked at Weasel, and then down at her badge and uniform, her duty belt with her Glock. She took one last look at Weasel, and headed for the door.

Chapter 18

Nicole didn't feel self conscious in her new uniform – she was just too tired. She knew she shouldn't doze, but it was too hard to keep her eyes open. Weasel was sedated next to her, his heart monitor drumming a steady beat. She closed her eyes and saw the man with the gun in Fort Rock, only this time he had five others with guns with him. She brought her gun up, and shot the man as he was shooting Weasel, and the others started shooting, and then the screaming began.

She shook her head and opened her eyes, bewildered, shaking her head. Weasel was where she had just left him, and she looked down at her uniform. Of course, now she remembered. The Indian Health Services. IHS. The screaming was coming from the hallway. She took one last look at Weasel, opened the large door, and stepped into the hall.

Down the hall by the glass front of the clinic, a tribal officer was trying to restrain a tall man with long black braided hair and sleeved tattoos on both arms. A woman was trying to hit the officer and screaming. Nicole ran toward the officer as Doctor Semington stepped out from a side door and walked to the struggle. Nicole went past him and started talking to the woman as she approached.

"Hey, come here, talk to me."

The woman was middle aged, with grey and black hair, and wore a sleeveless dress and tennis shoes. Her face was contorted and red from screaming.

"We only took a little," She screamed, and tried to hit the officer again. Nicole reached over and took her hand and pulled her away, talking to her softly, leaning in so the woman would have to stop yelling to hear.

"Wha-?"

"Come here, talk with me." Nicole pulled her further away.

"We just needed a little bit," she said, her voice now a plaintive whine, the screaming gong. She looked past Nicole and her shoulders slumped. Doctor Semington came up and put his hands on her shoulders.

Nicole looked over and saw that the officer and the tall Indian were just standing and looking at her and the woman. A girl of about ten sat on the bench beside the entry way, clutching a worn stuffed figure to her mouth, a doll, Nicole thought. Big brown eyes and black hair, jeans, a black and orange jacket, T-shirt. The doll covered most of her face.

She's watching her parents. OhmiGod!

"Nancy," Semington said, softly, bending down and looking into the woman's eyes. She lifted her head up.

"Nancy, I will authorize enough for a few days. We don't know what's going to happen, but Victoria will be on the top of the list for distribution, I promise. Okay?"

Nancy leaned against Nicole and started sobbing, and Nicole did the only thing she could do, she put her arms around the woman and led her to a bench. She caught Semington's eyes over Nancy's shoulder, and he was nodding. Yes.

Semington went over to the man, and the man reached into his pocket and held out two vials of liquid. Semington talked with him in low tones, and placed his hand around the man's hand, and closed his fingers around the vials.

"Keep them as cold as you can," Semington said. He took one more look at Nicole, and walked back to the ER.

Nicole saw the girl watching her, and went over and sat next to her. "Hi. I'm Nicole. I just got here." The little girl nodded. Nicole started to speak again, and the girl moved the doll.

"I'm Victoria," she said, her eyes never leaving Nicole's face.

"I am happy to meet you, Victoria. And who is this?"

"That's my doll, Crazy Horse. He was a great warrior."

"I know, and thank you for showing him to me."

Victoria looked up and saw that her parents were leaving. She stood up and stood in front of Nicole. "You're that pilot lady, Weasel's woman." And she walked toward the door.

Nicole started to say something, and then it was too late.

Semington waved the parents to the doors. They put their arms around Victoria, and the three of them left. As they got to the door, Victoria pulled the doll from her face and smiled, and then waved at Nicole. They walked outside, and were gone.

The officer came over and extended his hand. He was a Siyapu, a white man, and Nicole learned that about half of the tribal police department was non-Indian. He was young, with a ready smile.

"I'm Steve Fennel. I heard that you were a pilot, a nurse, and a deputy in California," he said. "That's quite impressive."

"Thanks," Nicole said, "I am a nurse, was a reserve deputy, and only a student pilot. Weasel was my instructor. I only managed to land the Cessna on the road."

"You and Weasel are the only two to ever do that," Steve said with a smile.

"Well, I had a good instructor."

"Are things as bad as we're hearing, the power out all over?" Steve said, the concern in his voice coming through, as if he could let some of the tension go with a fellow officer.

"Yeah, most likely. We flew from the L.A. area up here, all dark in the L.A. basin, the Bay Area, and southern Oregon. Everything. Gunshots starting last night when we left north L.A. area.

"Shit." I have a sister in the Monterey area." The worry was in his face, his voice.

"Well, hopefully she will hunker down, let the worst pass."

"Yeah," Steve said, looking at something she could not see, looking at a memory. He shook his head and then smiled.

"Well welcome aboard, Nicole." She shook his hand and thought she should check in with ER, when she saw

Semington open the door to ER and motion to her. As she started in that direction, Steve called out to her.

"Hey, nice to see that Weasel has a woman."

Damn. Does it ever quit here? I've been here a few hours, and the entire reservation believes that I'm Weasel's woman.

In spite of her tiredness, Nicole smiled at the thought. *What the hell? What else did you have planned for the rest of your life? And from the sounds of things last night in L.A., the rest of your life, girl, might just have been really short.* And then she had another thought. *Sure hope I can stay here, and being a nurse is gonna help. And they gave me a uniform. What the hell?*

Chapter 19

Semington was checking Weasel's dressing when Nicole came in. She stood in the doorway, and then moved slowly into the room, letting the double doors close behind her. In the quiet of the room, she could hear, feel, the throbbing of a generator somewhere outside. The room was bright with lights.

Weasel appeared to be awake, his eyes were open, blinking. He turned and looked at her.

He tried to talk and nothing came out. Nicole walked over and took his hand. He turned slightly and tried a smile.

"See you," he said, a croak. "See you got a uniform. You work fast lady."

"What can I say, I'm a city girl. My job is to guard the clinic and the resident pilot. You."

He said something she couldn't hear.

Semington moved to the door. "Call me if you need me," and he was gone, giving Nicole one last look. She thought she saw the beginnings of a smile from the tall doctor.

Nicole bent over Weasel. It came out as a whisper. "How did I get here?"

"We were flying up here in your plane after the lights went out in L.A. We landed in Fort Rock and you were shot."

"I, uh, remember L.A., you and I flying the helicopter, and then leaving, but what happened at Fort Rock? That's fuzzy."

"We got some gas cans, three men came up, one shot you, and I shot him. The rest ran off, and I got you in the plane and took off. You told me how to get here."

Weasel closed his eyes, and slightly shook his head. "You shot someone?" He said it softly, and opened his eyes. "You saved my life."

"Well, there wasn't much else to do," Nicole said.

"But how did we get here? In IHS? I know the doc from long ago, I could hear him talking as he was patching up my arm, but how did we get here, Nicole?"

"I landed your plane on the road." She smiled. "People tell me that you and I are the only ones to do that," and she laughed. Weasel tried to laugh, and winced. He looked serious. "Plane alright?"

"Of course," Nicole said with a smile. "I was the pilot in command."

"And look at you, a tribal police uniform, a nurse, and now a pilot."

"Yeah, I think they are going to keep me. Semington wants me around. I get to guard IHS and you and be a nurse." Nicole looked across the room, thinking, and made a decision. Quicker than she would have liked, but being around Weasel now made her feel good, made her tummy turn when she saw him. He saved her, and she in turn had saved him. She leaned over and kissed him on the lips and didn't make it a quick one. A kiss with feeling, with a smile, with a thank you. His eyebrows arched, and he squirmed a little, and then stopped. In the last second, he kissed back, his breathing coming fast.

"What was that for?" he whispered. She saw him follow her with his eyes as she stood up.

"For saving my ass," Nicole said. "I didn't know I would return the favor so soon, but it worked out. And," she said, leaning over again, inches from his face, "everyone on the Rez, and I mean everyone, refers to me as 'Weasel's Woman.'"

She heard a commotion in the hallway, and they both looked to the door. At least no one was screaming. She stood up and started that way.

"Nicole." Weasel was leaning forward, his shoulders off the bed, looking at her. She turned.

"Nicole," he said softly, "since you were speaking of saving your ass, I want you to know that I used to sneak a look at it when you were flying, during all those lessons. You have a fine ass."

She walked to the door. "You get better, mister. I have a feeling that they are going to need for us to fly soon, to see what's going on around us." She smiled. "You play your cards right, buster, you might just get to touch my ass." They both laughed as Nicole slipped out into the hallway.

She expected to see another fight, but the people who had been yelling were walking out, continuing to yell at each other. She looked down the hallway and it was nearly empty all the way to the pharmacy at the other end.

Semington waved to her from his office. She went in and he motioned to a chair. There was a picture of a woman with brown hair. Another picture had the four of them, Semington, wife, and two pre-teen kids. She didn't know him well enough to ask where they were.

He helped her out, pointing at the picture.

"My wife, Marilee, and Dan and Randy, my kids. They are here, we have a house here, probably safer than any other place I can think of, but it's going to get ugly."

She could feel the strain in his voice. He probably had as much sleep as anyone else around here.

"You're a nurse, so you know some of what we are going to face. The Indian population suffers from the highest rate of diabetes in the United States, maybe the world. Almost seventeen percent Type II, and about five percent Type I. The five percent is almost ten times the national average. That little girl, Victoria, in a month, or maybe two weeks, she will be gone, and there's not a damn thing I can do about it. Insulin, of which we have a pretty good supply, needs to be refrigerated, and we get a new shipment every week. Our supply will be gone in a few days, and if I can manage it, I will talk with the chairman and do some kind of triage, let those with multiple health problems slip away, and try to keep little girls like Victoria alive."

Semington turned to look out the window at the sagebrush and Juniper tree covered hills, the rimrock of Basalt above the trees.

He whispered, and then Nicole understood what he said.

" Keep them alive."

"What can I do, Doctor?"

"Call me Pete." He turned back and looked at Nicole. "You been a nurse how long?"

"Nineteen years."

"Surgery?"

"Yes, and just about everything else. Worked the floors at Santa Barbara General - then surgery, then cardio surgery. I worked as a reserve deputy for the past six years, something different and not so different to do. Took flying lessons from Len, then I learned just yesterday that his name is Weasel."

"You were there when he was shot?"

"Yeah." And Nicole found herself telling the story again, and the landing.

"You too, you close?" Semington asked, a neutral question.

"I think maybe, yeah, we will be. I hope I can stay here."

"Trust me, if I have anything to say about it, and I do, you have found a home. I can use you as a nurse full time, and you have other skills. And I think Weasel likes you, kept mentioning your name when he was under." Semington smiled, the first smile she had seen. The smile left his face, and he appeared to be looking at a ghost.

And maybe he is, Nicole thought. *Maybe he's seeing the ghosts to come.*

"Even if we have enough food, which we most surely won't, we have a population with kidney, liver, heart, lung, and a host of other organ failures at a high rate. Daily medication for many people. Those medications are going to run out very soon. Some will survive. Most of the sicker ones won't. And, many of them count on me as their doctor, as their friend. And I'm going to fail them."

He looked away again, the agony in his voice a palpable thing, and it hung there between them. She thought that if she had to work with a doctor, he was the one. He actually cared about his patients.

Nicole stood up and offered her hand to the doctor. He stood up, the fatigue in his face a hurtful thing. He held out his hand.

"Nicole Kennedy."

"Welcome, Nicole. I'm glad you are here. We'll make this fight together, along with a few other good people. Go take care of your man."

Nicole walked into the wide hallway, and for the first time since she had arrived, it didn't sound strange to hear of Weasel as "her man."

Chapter 20

Tribal Police Administration

Martin dozed at his desk. He had just closed his eyes for two minutes and heard yelling out in the administration area. He opened his eyes, knowing that he would never again be able to sleep for an entire night.

He gripped the arms of his chair and thrust himself up, stood for a moment to clear the dizziness, and walked out by his secretaries desk.

Johnnie Wahina was sitting in Jamie's chair. The front or his blue flannel shirt was covered in blood. He was about fifty, stocky, with long grey and black hair. He was a logger, Martin thought, working for Gilbert's logging crew, an all-Indian group. He lived in Simnasho, was from the Wasco tribe. He waved his arms, and then started sobbing, putting his face in his hands.

Sgt. Lamebull stood by him, and said, "Chief, you need to hear this, maybe the rest of the staff, Smokey and his people for sure."

"I'll get them here," Martin said, and then added, "Get Doc Semington or a nurse here, see what they can do for Johnnie." He walked to dispatch to see if they could round up the supervisors.

Ten minutes later, in the squad room, they had a serious group. Smokey, his wife and daughter, Lori, and the new nurse, Nicole, Weasel's woman. She was attending to Johnnie.

"Tell the chief what you told me," Lamebull told Johnnie.

"Simnasho has been taken over by a buncha gangsters, prison gang or some such thing. They kilt most everyone there in the middle of the night, and almost got me, but I ran into the woods. I got a ride from the Nestling family, found them over on Route 3."

"What do you mean, a gang?" Smokey asked.

"I mean I heard them talking, they got bikes, vans, pickups, and a lot of guns. They are all from prison. Not really a biker gang. They came in and started killing, and maybe raping the women. They have the roads sealed. Set up in the fire hall and the longhouse. Burned some of the houses. "

"I have family there," Lori said, her eyes on fire. "And I'm gonna go there and kill all of them. Right now!"

Martin grabbed her arm, and said to her and the assembly.

"Not right now, we will get a lot of people killed."

Lori jerked her arm away and glared at her husband. "Not your people," she yelled, and stalked out of the room. Martin looked after her, and then turned to the group.

"Johnnie, how many you think there were?"

"Uh, hard to say, chief, maybe forty, maybe more. They had vans, trailers, pickups. They looked like they was gonna stay for awhile. And as I was running for the trees, I heard two loud gunshots from Martha's house, like a large rifle."

Smokey smiled a grim smile.

"She has a 44-40 pistol, and a 44-40 rifle boss. Knows how to use them. My bet is on her."

Martin couldn't imagine the frail elder woman using a hand cannon like the 44-40, but he wouldn't put anything past the abilities of Martha Couer d'Alenes.

"Where would she go?"

"She would go into the woods, then take an old trail that parallels Hwy 3, all the way to the river. There is an old ford on the river, the old ones know about, she could stay out of sight of the road all the way to upper dry creek. She'll have rounded up survivors, and will head this way."

"How long?"

"She'll be in upper dry creek sometime late tonight. I'll put a patrol out there early evening, maybe have someone start that way on horseback, intercept them. They'll have the intel we need."

"Can we block Simnasho?"

"Already started thinking about it. I have some ideas for harassing and blocking." Smokey looked toward the door, a group of people standing there, trying to get in. He turned back to Martin, and said softly, "After we block them, they won't leave there alive. Just so you know, Boss."

Martin nodded. They were in a war for their survival.

George Wolfhead had been waiting just outside Martin's office. Martin waved to the gang leader. George came in and stood inside the door. He raised his hand, and Martin thought of being in school. He pointed.

"George, you got something to say."

"I just heard about Simnasho. Those are my people. You said that I had to be on your side. Well here I am. With some of my homies. Use us."

He stood there with his massive arms folded. He glared at the people in the room.

Martin nodded to Smokey. "Lt. Kukup's the tactical commander of all of the forces in Cold River. He will use you in a way that works, right, Smokey?"

Time to make peace, Smokey. And I hope you do.

Smokey walked over and held out his hand. George took it, and followed Smokey out of the room.

Bluefeathers arrived and then things got interesting.

Chapter 21

Smokey led George and seven of his gangbangers, all tribal members, to his office. He started without preamble.

"I want Hwy 3 blocked, a mile from Simnasho, or whatever place suits you. Maybe two miles to the west, in the canyon, good place for an ambush. Two miles to the north, and to the south, toward Kah Nee Ta, block it somewhere around Schoolie Flats. Use your imagination."

"Blocked how," George said.

"Physically block the road, trees, cars, whatever you can find. If they get past, I want them on foot. Keep them there, and keep reinforcements from joining them. Block Hwy 3 at Hwy 26 as well. But, I don't want them to get to Kah Nee Ta, to get closer to here."

"What about food, water, like that?"

"Take what you have, live off the land for a time. Do you need armament? Guns?" It bothered Smokey to give them guns.

"I think we're good with guns," George said, and smiled.

"Get a radio from dispatch. The battery won't last long, so only turn it on when you need to report. Dispatch will monitor 24/7. Have a runner in each group so you can communicate with each other. If you find survivors, have them make their way to the Agency, or have them join you."

"Smokey," George said. "Can we kill them? These people who took over Simnasho?"

Tribal Police Lieutenant Smokey Kukup gave his arch enemy, the 18th streeter gang leader and ex-con a grim smile, and said, "All you want. Just don't let them get past you."

George grinned then and shook Smokey's hand. "You can count on both things, Lieutenant Smokey. There will be some killing, and they won't get past us. Not alive anyway."

"And, George, use your own judgment, but I would like to see you make some harassing probes every couple of nights, from different directions, snipe a couple and then pull back. I want them off balance and afraid to close their eyes. If they come at you in force, pull back and snipe them. You must contain them until we have time and people to go up there and remove them."

"Roger that, Lieutenant." The large tattoo-covered former federal prisoner smiled again. "And, we get to kill as many as we want."

"Yes, and if you find tribal members, others up there, you guys take care of them. Get them here safely."

Smokey thought later that he had never seen George smile before. Not like that anyway. Smokey was about ready to unleash untold Hell upon a group of very bad people, in the form of George Wolfhead. Now on the side of the good guys.

Chapter 22

Indian Head Mountain

Gopher was growing into his new role as a man, Martha saw, and she deferred to his decisions, even if she would have done something differently. He had insisted that she ride the mare, and he and Cecilia distributed the contents of the bags to the people, the survivors from Simnasho. Throughout the night and during the day, their group had grown to twenty-one, a far cry from the four hundred residents who normally called Simnasho home. She knew that there would be many more out in the woods, and they would eventually make their way down to the Agency.

She groaned. They were going down the back side of Indian Head Mountain, on nothing more than a game trail. She looked over the country and knew that she had done the right thing when she shot the bad men. She had been born here on this land eighty-six years ago, and she would die to keep it. Riding the mare was almost as bad as walking. At least she could shift positions and move around as the mare walked. She reached down and patted her horse. She had been a good mare for a long time.

The mountain was mostly bare of trees at this elevation. She could see for miles, and if they kept this steady pace up, they would be at the river in an hour. With the low water, they could all walk across the old ford place. She knew that they didn't want to go over a mile to the east to the road. The bridge could be deadly, depending on who was there.

"We'll have water soon," she told her horse, and patted her sweaty neck. The grassy mountainside with spring flowers starting to come out was beautiful. Forest behind them, a river down below, and then the last hillside to walk up. If the situation had been different, she would have enjoyed the day. Now she took enjoyment in seeing Gopher.

He held his hand up as they got down to the river. He came back up to Martha, and took the halter rope.

"*Ala*, is this where we cross."

"Yes, grandson. And you have done a wonderful job of leading the people to safety." She smiled. "And your *Ala* is very proud of you." She reached in her pack and pulled out the heavy 44-40 ancient revolver. She handed it to Gopher. "You have shot before, remember to use two hands, to put the front sight blade on your target, and you have to cock the hammer on this one first." She spoke softly as she handed it to him, her on the horse, he at the water's edge. He leaned closer to hear. She touched his shoulder. "I'm very proud of you grandson. Now go lead our people." Gopher touched her shoulder, and stood up straight. He placed the revolver in his belt, and walked back to the head of the line. He stepped into the water.

Martha sat a little straighter in the saddle. Just yesterday her grandson was a child, a kid with long hair and an earring, and a fast car with loud music. Now he was a man, and becoming a leader.

I suppose that's how it always happens. We don't get leaders until we really need them. And now the people need you, you old woman. You have to teach them the old ways, the ways without electricity. Of tribal law and wisdom.

They made it to upper dry creek in the early evening. Gopher was still leading their little band, and that is how she thought of their group, their little band. The line spread up the hill behind them, children, toddlers carried by older children, teens, and middle-aged and elderly. They helped each other. There were three other horses, a mule, and some goats. They numbered about thirty now.

Martha looked across the hills to the Mutton Mountains. She imagined how the people had always traveled from danger – a line of tired, thirsty, and hungry people, leaving behind their dead, their missing, and fleeing as refugees in their own land. This has happened since time immemorial, she thought, *from Moses to Chief Joseph.*

To be sent running from her own house angered her to a point that her heart couldn't keep up, and she knew she had to stay calm. She was going to speak to the people, to the tribal council members, to the chiefs of the three tribes. She was going to go back to her home, if she had to take her guns and return alone.

When they got to Upper Dry Creek, they were met by a police officer, that Wewah boy, and several others.

When they crowded around, Wewah spoke. "There's going to be a meetin' tonight. At the agency longhouse. Chief Martin said that you would have survived, and for us to wait here for you. He thought you might take the old trails, and here you are."

They passed out water and snacks of jerky. There were cars waiting for them. The nine-mile trip to the Agency took just fifteen minutes, a distance that had taken them most of the day on foot. The *Siyapu* and their inventions were useful until they ran out of gas.

When they got to the Agency, things had indeed changed. And there was that meetin' for all who could make it from around the reservation. And what a meetin' it was.

Chapter 23

Mt. Wilson

"Dad, I don't see why I have to go to our home by Mt. Wilson? I helped you when we were kidnapped, remember? I just don't see--?

Smokey looked over at his daughter, and then back at the road. He had as much sleep as any of the others – maybe two hours. They had driven up the grade on Hwy 26, driving around stalled and wrecked cars and trucks. An officer was at the top of the hill, sitting with his overhead lights on, looking at traffic. It had slowed to a trickle. There must be a thousand predators between Portland and Mt. Hood, just north of the reservation. Dangerous thing, leaving your house when civilization collapses. He drove around a burned out car and went on for another mile and then turned west, toward Mt. Jefferson. At least now they were off the highway. They could take roads that would take them in and out of the timber all the way to the log house he and Jennifer and Laurel shared with his mother.

A large log house at the base of Mt. Wilson, a meadow in the front, and timber in the back.

A log truck was stopped in the road ahead. The driver got out and came back as Smokey slowed.

"Hi, Cecil," Smokey said.

"Smokey. Is it as bad as they say it is?

"Maybe worse. Power out all over the U.S. Oh, and Cecil, take some of these flyers. There is a meeting tonight at the Agency Longhouse, all people should come. Can you take some of these flyers and spread them around?"

Cecil held his hand out and put the flyer up to his face. In bold black print, the flyer said:

MEETING ABOUT ELECTRICITY AND OUR SURVIVAL

For All Tribal Members and Employees

7 p.m. Saturday April 24 Agency longhouse

Make it to the meeting any way you can. Buses will be at the following pickup points (except Simnasho) at 6p.m. Sidwalter, Countyline Road. The meeting will be broadcast in Sahaptin on KWSO for those who can't make it. Food provided.

Cecil took a handful and looked at the flyer again. "Uh, Smokey, I can get to all the people up here off County Line Road, and up as far as Sidwalter. That be okay?"

"That will work, and Cecil?"

The logger leaned in the window.

"Tell people to carry a gun, will you?" Smokey said. "We are gonna be in a fight to keep the reservation if this keeps up. I will organize our fight, but I want everyone ready to go."

Cecil clasped Smokey's arm. "That last thing on the paper, about food provided, that'll get them there." He looked closely at Smokey. "You think it will come to that?"

Smokey nodded. "Simnasho's already under assault. This is serious, Cecil."

The logger nodded, and walked back to his truck.

Smokey took the back roads, turned on the B100 road, and they met two other people on the road, and in each case they were given a handful of flyers.

They were at the log house in another twenty minutes.

His mother had lived there at the edge of the wilderness area for sixty years. She was the most self-sufficient person he knew. He and Laurel and Jennifer lived there as well, although they had a duplex down in Cold River.

They used the duplex during the school year and when Smokey had late nights at the department. Jennifer was comfortable in either place, and was very close to Smokey's mother. He had wanted Jennifer and Laurel to be at the house in the woods in case things got worse, and to take care of his mother, not that she needed it.

Smokey drove down the half-mile drive, over a small wooded hill and into the meadow. The house sat back almost to the trees, the mountain rising up behind it. The new log structure was imposing. A barn and corals were off to the left, with four horses, a large haystack, and a shed. There was a new SUV parked in front of the house. A slight stream of smoke drifted out of the chimney.

As they pulled up, his mother came out the front door and waited. Laurel ran to her when the car stopped.

Smokey put his arm around Jennifer.

"I don't like this, husband," she said. She liked using the idiom of the Indians, calling him the deferential "husband."

"This is better. I will be here soon. I have a radio for you, keep it charged on the generator. Check in with dispatch for a few seconds each night." He leaned over for a kiss and when it didn't come, he said softly, "it's my job to protect my family, and this is best, and I will worry about you and Laurel, but you will be safer here. Let me do my job as a husband."

Jennifer touched his face, and then kissed him, and touched her stomach. "Him too, he will be safe here."

He gathered them in the living room. The room was filled with artifacts of the past, some donated from friends, other tribal members. The kitchen had a modern wood stove, one his mother used every day. They would do well here without electricity. They had adequate food stored, and his mother put up food the old way, using drying racks and vegetable mounds. They could turn the horses out in the meadow for feed. His mother sat bedside him. He took her hand in his. Jennifer sat on his right side, holding on to his arm.

"Mom, you know the electricity has gone off, probably around the country. There will be a lot of death, and I think you all will be safe here. I have work to do at the Agency, to fight bad people who will come, some who are here."

"We'll be okay, with Jennifer and Laurel, we will be fine."

"You have a base radio here, charge the batteries every few days with the generator, check in with dispatch every evening, I will try to talk for a minute." He said this to Laurel and Jennifer. Laurel sat across from him, a scowl on her face. He looked at her. "You know things. I want you to tell me what you see when you have an idea. Okay?"

She nodded, sullen.

"Put the dogs out, you will know if they are barking at a deer or at a person. And Laurel, Jennifer, carry your guns everywhere, even if you are going to the barn. Everywhere, okay?" Even at Laurel's age, she had used a gun before to protect herself and Jennifer. Smokey knew that if it came to it, she would again.

"There are some bad people now in Simnasho, and it will take us a while to clear them out. I don't think they will venture this far, we will have blockers in place soon, but if they do, the three of you get into the woods off the back deck. They can't find you there. You can make your way to the agency. Laurel." She looked up.

"Laurel, you and Jennifer and mom put some supplies and packs and ammunition up in the woods by my sweat lodge, just in case you have to run up there."

Laurel nodded. They all knew it could happen. Laurel spoke, this time more animated, a plea to go with him.

"Okay, Dad, but I still think I could help down at the Agency. I can tell you things, you know?"

He reached for her, and she came and stood before him. He hugged her. "You know I need you to stay here and take care of your Ala, Jennifer, and your baby brother."

Laurel nodded. Reluctant.

Smokey stood and led Jennifer outside. At the truck, he kissed her and touched their baby.

"Bye, my husband. Come back to us." Jennifer looked as if she were going to cry, but didn't. She kissed Smokey again, and stood there as he got into the truck. Smokey turned around the drive and looked back as he drove slowly through the meadow. Laurel and his mother had joined Jennifer. His heart ached with worry, but he was a warrior, and he needed to put together a force to protect his people, the reservation. He had more current combat experience than anyone here and he was going to use it with deadly efficiency. Smokey looked back at the log house at the edge of the woods one last time.

Police Lieutenant Smokey Kukup, tribal member and army ranger veteran of the Afghan wars, never saw the log house again. He made it back to the Agency in an hour, handing out flyers to everyone he met.

Laurel stood in front of the house and watched her father drive away. She knew he had to go, but she also knew she could help at the Agency. On the reservation, age didn't matter as much as on the outside. Eighteen and Twenty-one meant nothing. Even though she was ten she was a Twixtli, a person the whites called "Shaman" and she couldn't help it as much as she could stop breathing. Her dad had fought it until she had saved him and Jennifer and others. Now he just didn't talk about it much. After they saw the upside down plane and the white fox, she knew that this was the start of a very dark period. And she knew of some of the bad things about to happen, but she couldn't see it all yet.

And when she was able to see what was to come, she was afraid that it would be too late for many of them. The one thing she did know for sure she didn't tell her dad. The bad men were coming for them at their house at the edge of the woods.

By the time the bad men were there, it was too late to tell him.

Chapter 24

Agency Longhouse, 6:00 p.m.

Lori sat in the backseat of Martin's Tahoe, leaning between the seats. Martin was in the driver's seat, Smokey in the passenger. They were parked outside in the lot, near the east side, watching. Even though the meeting wasn't due to start for an hour, the parking lot was half full, and people were coming from all directions – in cars and trucks, on foot, on horseback, and she had even seen a mule. Some were dressed traditional, some in flannel shirts, and a few in suits. The one thing that made this different from other general meetings was the armament. Almost every one, or at least someone in every family, was armed, from pistols and revolvers, to hunting rifles, to AR rifles, to black powder guns. She saw several crossbows, and traditional bow and arrow outfits. She had never seen anything like it.

The largest concentration of people was on the north side, where the elders had set up a large open air tent, and were cooking traditional meals. Nothing like food to get people to come. Especially now, when it might run out at some point.

She and Martin had not spoken since she had angrily yelled those hurtful words at him in the conference room, and she was hurting so bad for having said those words that she felt like crying.

Not now, Lori. You can't cry now. You must talk with him.

They had the overhead lights flashing on top of the SUV, a way Smokey thought to let people know that there was still order here. For the most part, they were ignored. Lori saw people she had known since childhood. A few waved at her, and she waved back. She had not been wearing a uniform since she had started to show in her pregnancy, but everyone knew she was an officer, just the same. Martin and Smokey wore tribal police uniforms.

"How many people will the longhouse hold?" Martin asked.

"On a night like tonight, maybe a thousand. There's the basketball court, and bleachers all around, and room in the back. But that is all the room we will probably need. Many families will only send one representative, some will bring everybody."

Lori looked over at the road from the west hills housing area and saw people moving together, walking as a group. Slouching was more like it, she thought. She pointed.

"Look what we have here." Martin and Smokey followed her arm.

"Damn," Smokey said. "They're all dressed up with no place to go."

"NGT." Martin said. A statement not a question. Lori knew he was very familiar with them. A gang to rival any intercity gang, with affiliates on many reservations. NGT. Native Gang. At war with the 18th Streeters. And any other gang on the Rez. They were about a dozen in all, and Lori knew all of them. She opened her door and stepped out, followed by Martin and Smokey.

She led them, and walked up to the approaching group. The leader, Tommy, stopped as she approached. He wore a sleeveless T-shirt, had long black hair, high cheekbones colored with tattoos, in fact his arms were sleeved in tattoos. Gang tats, jail tats. He carried an AR15 in a sling and a bandolier of magazines, the thirty-round kind she thought, in another sling.

I see the slouch, Tommy, the slouch of a seventeen-year-old armed to the teeth. And your pants need pulling up. You might be a big tough native gangbanger, but you have adopted the slouching of inner city fucks like you.

"Tommy," Lori said it evenly, waiting to see what was about to play out.

"Officer Lori Andrews. You know my name now is Keelah, for killer. Only my family calls me Tommy." He nodded at Martin, acknowledging Lori's last name. He grinned at Smokey. "Lieutenant."

"Going to the meetin' I see," Lori said.

"Gonna do our part," Keelah said. Even though he was seventeen, he was the undisputed leader of the NGT. There were bangers in the group older, but he was the leader. As Tommy once put it to Lori, you had to be a "skin" to get into the gang.

"We are going to make you the same offer we made to the 18th Streeters," Lori said.

At the mention of the 18 streeters, anger flared in his face. "We'll take care of George, those fucks when this is over," Keelah said, his voice rising, fairly yelling at the end. He took a breath. "They got one coming. We'll be coming around for that one."

He spit on the ground. He waved his arms at his group. "NGT means Native, you know? Fuckin' Native. We have native in our gang. George, with the gang name from L. fucking A., that's full of some In-dins, Mexicans, *Siyapu*," and as he said this he glared at Martin, "and he even has c'*mukly* (black) members, from some prison gang bullshit or other." He thumped his chest.

"We're NGT."

"Got it," Lori said dryly.

"We need for your group to guard both dams, the river between the dam and the bridge. You can select your group, but we need twenty-four/seven guards in that area." She waited and watched Tommy.

"As long as the Streeters aren't involved, we will do it."

Martin spoke for the first time.

"You need weapons?" Lori knew he wasn't offering, but more like gathering information about what they had.

"We can always use more, but nah, I think we're good." He touched the AR and smiled. "When do we start?"

"As soon as the meeting is over," Lori said. "And, you will report to Lt. Kukup for assignment and rules." She saw the look on Tommy's face, and added, "Yes, Tommy, rules."

Keelah leered at Smokey and nodded, and the group walked toward the food tables. Tommy was followed by a girl of about fifteen. She carried a baby. They stood and watched the NGT gang as they moved toward the longhouse.

"Jesus." Smokey said. "We're gonna have trouble with that one."

"My sentiments exactly," Martin said.

"See you two in a bit," Smokey said, waved at a family, and walked to them.

Lori turned to Martin. "Can we go to the car for a minute, husband?"

Martin gave her a look, and they walked to the Tahoe. He held her door open for her, and she gave him a sad, brief smile.

Lori got in the passenger side of the Tahoe and Martin quietly shut the door. She looked straight ahead, and for all of her strength, her ability to be in people's faces, her alpha female qualities, a tear rolled down her cheek, and then a flood started. The sun was starting to slide down behind Mt. Jefferson, and the scene outside was blurred. Tears ran down her face and dropped on her jeans. She could feel Martin turn to her, and he put his arm around her and pulled her to him. She threw her arms around him and put her face in his neck and sobbed as he held her.

Martin waited, and that was just one of the things she so dearly loved about him. She tried to speak, and no words came out. She tried again, her lips on his neck, and then she spoke.

"Husband. I'm so . . . so sorry."

He nodded and rubbed her neck.

"I'm so ashamed," she whispered. "I treated you badly and without honor or respect. I hurt you, and am so appalled. Can you ever forgive me?"

He started to say something, and then was silent.

Lori began talking again, her voice low, husky with emotion. "You have risked your life for my people, now your people, and for your daughter-to-be." Lori pulled back from his neck and looked into his eyes from inches away.

"You are my warrior," she whispered, and the tears started again. "Please forgive me, husband."

Martin wiped the tears away with his thumbs, and smiled. His smile broke Lori's heart, the love, the tenderness. This man she loved, this husband. She had acted so badly as a wife. An Indian wife.

"Husband."

Martin looked at her face.

"Husband, do you still love me?"

He kissed her, a tender slow kiss, and then, full of emotion. He pulled back and smiled. "Of course, Lori, my beautiful love, I will always love you." She nodded, ready to cry again.

"One of the things I love about you is your passion, your sense of right and wrong." He held her face away a few more inches, and smiled. "You were so angry at invaders taking your homeland, killing your friends, that you wanted to go take them out instantly. You didn't want to wait for anyone or anything. My little warrior, I know where your heart was, and where it always is between us."

She threw her arms around him, and felt him stiffen, and then she heard it. There were gunshots to the northeast of them, down by the bridge across the river she thought, and then a lot of them.

"I love you," Martin whispered. "As long as I am chief of police, and your husband, I have work to do." He kissed her again, and opened his door. Lori smiled, feeling more relieved than she had all day, the sickness of having said those awful words to her husband fading away.

"Thank you, Husband. And, Martin, don't forget you still have to do as I say." He nodded and laughed, and called for Smokey. She opened her door to help. The shooting she could deal with. Dishonoring her husband and hurting him – that she could never abide again.

Chapter 25

Smokey was talking on a portable radio as Martin and Lori walked up, a luxury Martin thought would end one day soon.

"A pickup wouldn't stop on the bridge, rammed one of our cars, the driver and occupants opened fire on our officers. Officers had cover, they are okay. Two of the invaders they let run away. Two others dead."

Invaders, Martin thought. *That's how we are thinking of people not from here now, and I guess it's as good of a term as any.*

"Do they need us there?"

"No, Sergeant Lamebull and Walker are going down, going to beef up the roadblock. That's the only bridge onto the Rez for a lot of miles. We knew some people would try it, and it will only get worse when people get hungry."

Lori pointed. "Chairman's here. Maybe we should go inside, he wants us and Doctor Semington with him. Lori looked over the sidewalk and saw Nicole, holding onto a pale looking Weasel. They had walked from the IHS clinic, two blocks away. Lori motioned for the nurse and pilot to join them.

"How are you, Nicole?" And then Lori looked at Weasel. "And how are you, Weasel?"

Weasel muttered something.

"He's grouchy," Nicole said, "but I'm used to that, I'm a nurse."

Lori laughed. "Come with us, the chairman is going to say some words about you, Weasel, and you, Nicole. This is going to be a long night.

They heard more gunshots to the west as they entered the auditorium. Yes, this was going to be a long night.

The bleachers were full and the basketball floor was filled with chairs, families on blankets, people standing. There was a podium under the basket on the north end. The emergency lights were on, giving a dim light to the arena, light that would fade as the batteries ran low. Lori knew she would know most of the people in the room. She nodded as they made their way to the podium, and stood to the side.

A generator came to life outside, and the podium was lighted with two lamps. The microphone came to life with a whine. Jim Fast Horse walked onto the stage and adjusted the microphone. He held up his hands, and tested the mic.

"People of Cold River, please observe a silence while elder Mary Ramsey says a prayer.

Mary walked slowly into the light, her figure slight, bowed. Lori could see her bright eyes from where she stood.

Mary began singing a prayer in Sahaptin, her voice soft, and then rose in pitch, a beautiful, mournful sound, and Lori felt like crying for the fourth time today.

Must be the pregnancy hormones, yes, that's what it is.

When Mary finished, the auditorium was quiet, except for the crying of a baby. Chairman Bluefeathers walked slowly into the light, his body erect, his head held up. He wore his usual outfit – new flannel shirt, jeans, cowboy boots, long braided hair, a leather and bead necklace, and he carried a warrior's lance.

As he approached the mic, the crowd began clapping and people stood, a few at first, and then the entire auditorium was on its feet, the noise thunderous, people clapping, yelling, stomping. Lori could feel the bleachers shake, the air trembled.

Bluefeathers held his hands up. The clapping and stomping and yelling slowed, and then suddenly stopped.

Bluefeathers waited for a long fifteen seconds, and then said one word.

"Ai." (Hello)

The auditorium roared, and to a person they held up their right hand in greeting, and repeated, "*Ai.*"

He waited again, ten seconds this time.

"I come to you in a time of great danger to our people. As you know by now, the electrical grid in the United States had gone down, by what means, we do not know. Probably by our enemies. That means a great deal to us, for us to survive as a people, as a nation. I also want to say that this talk is being broadcast on KWSO in Sahaptin, so those around us won't know what we are planning, what we are doing, but those tribal members who could not be here can be a part of this event."

Bluefeathers looked over the crowd. The auditorium in this sacred building, the Agency Longhouse, was mostly dark. In the dim light he could see the hundreds of eyes upon him. In the back a baby wailed, and then subsided as the mother took the child to a door. He paused for a few more seconds, and then took a deep breath.

"We have become weak!" It came out as a shout, and he meant it to be so. There were murmurs of agreement in the crowd.

"We have become dependent on the White's handouts, the food stamps, the government assistance, the welfare, the BIA subsidies, the exemption from taxation that our sovereignty gives us. Even now in this crowd, there are those of us who are wonder who will provide our next meal."

He paused again, and this time the room was silent. He knew that his words would either inspire the people to survive, or they would grow weaker and die. He said a quiet prayer to the Creator to give him the right words to say.

"In order to survive, from this point forward, everyone on the reservation, tribal member, Indians from other tribes, even Siyapu, will be governed by tribal law." His voice rose at the end, again almost a shout.

This time the entire crowd came to their feet, yelling, clapping, hooting. Bluefeathers waited, giving them time to bring it down. When he spoke again, he did so quietly.

"Many things have changed. The gas trucks are not coming. The food trucks are not coming. We can't go to Safeway or Thriftway in Madras with our food stamps or cash cards every day. That is gone. The electricity we are using for this event, to power this microphone, things we take for granted, they are gone after this time.

"We have as a people have the patience of a baby spilyay (coyote) much like the Siyapu. We will use the wisdom of our elders, and find the patience that it takes to grow food for a year, to hunt, to fish, to gather berries, to dig roots, to live and survive like we did with the old ways."

They had more patience than the *Siyapu*, but not much. They would have to learn tribal wisdom and patience again. For now, many were as patient as a baby *spilyay.*

"I am calling on everyone in this room, and to those listening around the reservation, to step up and be a part of the tribal solution, not to be a part of the problem." Bluefeathers had a lot more to say, but he knew that they could only absorb so much. He wanted to give it to them in little bites.

"Everyone on the reservation will work. You don't work, you don't eat. The Elders will contribute with their wisdom, their guidance for work crews in food gathering and preservation. Many of you have already volunteered. Even now we have guards on the borders. We have volunteers at IHS, at the community center, at the rodeo arena, guarding trucks, at the administration building, guarding the council and tribal chiefs. We have a lot more to do. And –"

He paused, and was going to take a break from speaking, to let other managers talk, but he had a lot more to say.

"*And,*" Bluefeathers lowered his voice to almost a whisper, his voice carried throughout the crowd with the sound system. *"And, many of you in this room and on this reservation will not be here a year from now. I wish it wasn't so, but even with our best efforts, we will lose some of our revered elders, and others among us. But we will save everyone we can. I want to turn this over to a man who means a great deal to our country, has devoted his life to our reservation, Dr. Semington."*

Bluefeathers stepped back from the microphone, and motioned to the shadows behind him. Semington stepped forward and Bluefeathers put his arm around him. As Semington stepped up to the microphone, someone in the back of the room yelled, "The whites must go!"

Bluefeathers stepped in front of Semington, and leaned into the mic, his face contorted. He yelled.

"Do you want our only doctor to go?" He waved his arm in an arc to include Semington. Most people in the crowd responded, yelling "NO!"

"I have something to say about the Siyapu here on the reservation. Many are married to tribal members, many work here. Some have died protecting, trying to rescue tribal members. Our Chief of Police, Martin Andrews, is married into the tribe, and he risked his life to rescue my granddaughter and other tribal members in a foreign land. We are not at war with the whites!"

The last came out as a yell again, and he knew he needed to calm down. It wouldn't do his tribe any good for him to have a heart attack or a stroke. He believed that he was in his position to lead his tribe out of danger.

There were murmurs of agreement again, and although he knew this would come up again, he hoped to quell some of it. He was going to stop, but he needed to say more.

When the room quieted, he started again. The room was growing dimmer, almost dark, but he could feel every eye on him.

"If we make war with the whites, and others, when this is over we will not survive as a nation. When the Great White Father in Washington, D.C., and the congress, hears of our war, they will come with force and occupy us. We all know that, and our neighbors up there in Madras, many of them are our friends, we went to school with them. If individuals or families try to cross our borders, we will turn them away, we will not hurt them, they are just hungry."

Bluefeathers knew now why the Creator had put him in this place. There were others on council who would make war. He knew that it was the wrong thing to do. They needed the *Siyapu* more than the *Siyapu* needed them. The room was quiet, with a few quiet conversations when he stopped. He took a deep breath, knowing that his people needed to hear what he was about to say.

"But, if anyone comes in force, to invade," and he rose his voice again with strength, *"If anyone, no matter who they are, comes to invade . . . we . . . will . . . kill . . . them!"* He literally yelled the last four words, and the crowd came to their feet again. He had hoped to save that for the end, but now he knew what he would say at the end. He held his hands up, and the room fell silent.

"We will take a ten minute break, those of you who didn't get to eat, go do so now, and then return quickly,

we have a lot of things to cover." He held his hand up, and said, *"Ai."*

Martin realized that as well as not sleeping much for the last forty-eight hours, he hadn't eaten as well. He and Lori and Smokey were standing in the darkness, beside the stage. People passing him were nodding, not unfriendly, some patted him on the arm. He knew that the talk about the whites was coming – he had been in general meetings before, although not at such a time as this. He had expected the talk from Bluefeathers, but wasn't sure how it would come out. Bluefeathers was an enigma at times. Martin never quite knew what the tribal leader was going to say. He had his arms around Lori, and she had her hands on his biceps.

"Lori."

"Hmm?"

"Do you think we could get something to eat out there where the elders are serving?"

"Of course, let's go and feed my husband." She looked down at her stomach, "and this little one here."

She took Martin's hand and they moved through the crowd. Many people smiled at Lori, and Martin as well. When they got outside they made their way to the tables with food. There were big stock pots with soup and stew. As Martin picked up a ladle to fill two bowls, Ken Blue put his arm on Martin's shoulder. He smiled at Martin.

"Dig deep, White Man, puppy's on the bottom."

Martin laughed. Lori poked Blue with her knuckle. "Get outta here, old man. Can't you see I'm feedin' my man?" She moved her hip into Blue, a friend of theirs who ran the forestry program, and shoved him out of the way. "I'm not feedin' him no puppy."

At least not yet, anyway, Martin thought.

Blue put his arm around Martin's shoulders, and hugged him tight. "Glad you're here, my friend." He looked into Martin's face, and moved away.

Me too, my friend. Me too.

He found a place to sit at a picnic table, and he and Lori ate in the dim light until the call to go back into the meeting came from someone in the doorway.

Semington was talking when they walked back in and took their place by the side of the raised platform. Bluefeathers had told Martin that he might want him to speak, and Martin had decided if that were the case, he would take Lori to the microphone with him. He just wouldn't tell her until it was too late for her to back out.

Semington talked of the illnesses on the reservation, the limited supply of medicine, and that he and the staff would do everything possible to keep the community healthy.

"You all know me," he said, with what Martin thought was affection in his voice. "I've spent much of my medical career here, and this is where I will stay. This is my home and calling, to help this tribe and its people." Martin thought that Bluefeathers was the only one who could get applause, but there was a hearty round of applause for Semington. The doctor continued. "The chairman has said that I could introduce a tribal member who has returned to us in his usual fashion – a dramatic fashion. I want to introduce my friend and our pilot, Weasel." Semington waved behind him, and as Weasel stepped into the light, the crowd roared. Weasel had his arm in a sling, and was supported by Nicole. She was still in her tribal uniform. Weasel raised his good arm from Nicole's shoulder and the noise continued.

"I also want to introduce someone who will be a very important person in this community." Semington touched Nicole on the arm, a gesture of support and friendship.

"Nicole Kennedy protected Weasel on the flight here. She shot the man who shot Weasel, and then she safely landed the plane here, a plane that will be very important to us in the future. Equally as important, Nicole is an experienced surgical nurse, and I will use her skills to help save the lives of people in this community. She will be helping the tribal police to guard our supplies and keep us safe at IHS."

A smattering of applause came from the crowd.

Semington held his hands up. "I also just found out . . . that she is Weasel's woman."

With that the crowd clapped and laughed, and Nicole blushed. Weasel grinned. They walked back into the darkness behind the podium, and Semington continued.

Martin watched and thought that the old Devil, Bluefeathers, sure did know how to orchestrate a meeting. There could have been resentment toward Nicole, her being here, eating tribal food, and a newcomer to the police department. Bluefeathers, with having Semington introduce her, made her a part of the community, for all but the few hard-core white haters. He had learned that Nicole's heritage was Mexican, but for those who didn't like the whites, she was a *Siyapu*. Not Indian. Semington finished, and waved. He got another large appreciative applause.

Bluefeathers came back, and brought Bobby Red Deer, the manager of Natural Resources. They had decided that Natural Resources would oversee the distribution of food and water, of hunting, of gathering and cutting firewood. A large job, that would need a lot of volunteers.

As Bobby came to the microphone, there was a noise from the back of the room, a buzzing, a lot of talking. He looked up, and those in front could see a slight figure walking down the center aisle of the basketball court.

Martin knew who it was from the way she walked.

Martha Couer d'Alenes, how are you, my dear, and my supporter, my nemesis. I am glad you made it here alive. He pointed for Lori. "Martha." Lori looked over his shoulder.

People were starting to stand, calling out to her. She was halfway up the aisle, and people all around were standing, and then clapping, then yelling, "Martha, Martha!" When she got to the front, Bluefeathers and the rest of the tribal council and the three tribal chiefs were there to meet her.

You old dog, Martin thought, *you old conniving tribal council chairman, you couldn't have orchestrated this better if you had been a philharmonic conductor. You brought her here in just the right moment, the right time. Of course, Bluefeathers, you could have had nothing to do with this, but if she arrived by car, you had a play in it. You don't leave anything to chance.*

Chief Colton of the Wasco tribe led her up to the stage. Martin knew, as did virtually everyone in the room, that Simnasho was the center of the Wasco Tribe, and at one time, had been the site of the government of Cold River.

Martha walked slowly to the microphone. She allowed the arthritis to show, and she limped with aching joints to the center of the stage. She carried her large bag with her, the strap around her shoulder.

"Ai."

The response was enormous. She waited, feeling the power of the people, and then she started to talk.

Chapter 26

Hwy 3, Three miles south of Simnasho

"Cars coming, George," Anthony said. He was the youngest of his men, just fifteen. They were boys. In the still of the evening he heard the engines just before he saw the headlights. The cars were coming from the north, from Simnasho. George had his people block the road at the southern end of a pass through the rocks, a passage of a hundred yards. If people tried to get through, they would have to retreat through a valley. The blockade wasn't much, three old cars parked nose to tail, but they should stop anything but a military vehicle or a bulldozer with a blade.

George whistled to his people. Indians for centuries began fighting as warriors at a young age. He had five with him; the rest of his group had established two other blockades – on Hwy 3 towards the road to Mt. Hood, and another to the west of Simnasho. He had only five boys on the Hwy to the north. He hoped they had enough. If they were assaulted in force, by men with a plan, he knew they wouldn't hold.

They took their places in the rocks, above the blockade of cars. He felt an excitement he hadn't felt in a long time. It was one thing to go to federal prison, to get out of prison and sell drugs, but he knew at some level that the *Siyapu* police chief had given him a way out, a way to live and die honorably. Sarah stood with him, holding her shotgun up at port arms, looking into the dark. George had an AR15 with two thirty-round magazines snapped together. He had six more in his vest. He could make war.

Joe, his second, had a similar AR, and was up in the rocks to their right. That position would put him on the driver's side of the approaching vehicles. Anthony, who had called out the approaching cars, was up with Joe. Up on the left, he had Jorge and Bonnie. They had placed a battery-operated million candle power spotlight up on each side of the road. If they used them sparingly, they might last for a few fights. He wanted to shock the invaders with the lights, and see what they would do.

"Three sets of headlights," Joe called from the rocks.

The lead car was a pickup, George saw, and slowed as it came up to the roadblock. His people had instructions to try to save the engines of the vehicles, so they could use them. If not, what the hell.

All three cars stopped, two pickups, and a van. At least six people he thought.

As the driver of the lead vehicle got out, both spotlights came on, showing a startled driver. The driver, a bearded man wearing a sleeveless T-shirt and a watch cap, pulled a shotgun out of the driver's seat. His arms were covered with crude prison tats.

"What the fuck is this?" The driver said, and swung the shotgun around and up and fired a shot at the spotlight above him, and all hell broke loose. George stepped beside the car on the end and fired a thirty-round magazine at the man, and then fired into the cab on both the driver and passenger side. Sarah opened up beside him with her pump twelve gauge, throwing out double ought buck rounds. He dimly saw the muzzle flashes from the rocks on both sides of the road.

George looked over his sights as he fired. The driver of the lead pickup danced, his chest and head exploding in a red mist, and he dropped as if the string of life had been cut, and it had.

The passenger of the lead vehicle suffered a similar fate, his body riddled with bullets as the gang opened up. Through the deafening roar of guns, George heard whoops, war cries, battle cries from another century.

The van in the rear was backing up, fast, and the defenders shot at the retreating headlights.

"Stop firing!" George yelled, and yelled again. "Let them go." He watched as the headlights of the van went out, first one, and then the other. The firing slowed, and then stopped.

"Turn off the spotlights!"

The lights went out, and darkness came to the road. At first there was no sound except for the retreating van, it's engine thrashing and knocking, and it went over a rise, and the sound retreated as well, and then it was quiet.

"Yeeeoooow," Joe yelled, and then the others took it up, and George let them go with it for a few more seconds.

"Cover them, Joe, from your side, Jorge, from your side. Let's not be stupid now, they might not be dead, be dangerous wounded animals. Everyone else, meet here with me."

They came down out of the rocks, Bonnie from the left, Anthony from the right, and joined George and Sarah. George turned on a flashlight, and with the group spread out beside him, they approached the driver of the lead pickup. He was indeed dead, most of his head and chest gone. The passenger suffered the same fate. They moved on to the second vehicle. Both the driver and passenger were dead, a man and a woman. The woman had turned to run back to the van and she was dropped at the back of the pickup.

"Should we go after the van?" Joe called. "That engine might not take them all the way back."

"No. This is better. I want the invaders in Simnasho to know that they are now in a war, it isn't going to be so easy for them. Jorge, Joe, join us down here. Bring the lights.

They met at the front of the blockade, and George gave his instructions. "Move the trucks out of the way."

Jorge checked the first one, and Sarah checked the second. Remarkably they both ran. "Put the bodies in the bed of one of the trucks. Jorge, you drive it part way back to Simnasho and park it in the road. Then run to the other roadblocks and see if they were challenged. Get back here as soon as you can. We'll be at our camp."

George heard a sound behind him, and turned to see Anthony, his body bent over, his rifle on the ground. The boy was sick. Not all of them were big tough gangbangers yet. But they all would be warriors soon. Oh, yeah, this was the first of many battles, of that he was sure.

"I'm proud of you, mano." George Wolfhead, the tough ex-con, tribal member, leader of the 18th street gang, put his arm around fifteen-year-old Anthony, and held him as he wretched. He had a feeling about this. A few days ago he would have ridiculed Anthony. He held him like a father would hold his sick little boy. George knew without putting it into words that he was changing from a loser gang member into something different. Maybe he was becoming a leader. A warrior, who leads and takes care of his warriors.

"You okay?" He asked Anthony, waving Sarah away when she came up.

Anthony nodded.

"Let's get you cleaned up. You fought well, Anthony. I would fight with you at my side any day." Anthony gave him a weak smile, and George could see the gratitude in his eyes. He patted the young warrior on the back, and walked him to the rest of their group.

What the hell am I doing? Whatever it is, I think I like it.

Tomorrow, George thought, they would take it to Simnasho.

Chapter 27

Cold River Rodeo Grounds

The semis were lined up side-by-side, end-to-end, and as far as Howard Kewa could tell, there were over a hundred of them. He had a crew of a dozen men and women and teens, and it was their job to guard and then inventory the trucks. They had been at it most of the day, and would continue into the night. People would come by and tell them what was happening in the longhouse, three blocks away.

He was checking a semi of what was mostly canned food, and his assistant, eighteen-year-old Vernon came up to him.

"Boss," he said, barely over a whisper. "Boss, Nancy told me to come get you, that you had to see this."

Howard knew better than to put him off, so he jumped down to the grass and followed the youngster into the night. There were several others crowded around the rear doors of a large trailer. They parted when Howard got there. He stepped on a small stool and shined his light into the interior of the forty-foot trailer.

He flashed the light again, just to be sure. *Jesus Christ on a crutch. What the hell?*

He had thought that the military would ship their equipment on military trucks. This truck was a plain brown wrapper, as they say.

Holy shit! Why would they do that, why would the military ship war material like this in a Swift, Inc. truck?

Maybe they did all the time and we just didn't know it. In any event, the chairman and the police chief have to know about this right away.

He looked around.

These kids aren't going to keep their mouths shut. We have to move this mother right away.

Howard looked again, and reached up, and closed the sliding door. "Get me a lock," he told Nancy. They had been putting their own locks on some of the trucks. He waited while she came up with a new lock and keys, and he jumped down and locked the door. He waved the group closer.

"Nobody talks about this, right?" They nodded. He looked at them. Shit, they had already put the word out. Some of them had already told their relatives. Gotta get to the chairman now.

"'Vernon. Nancy. Guard this truck. I'll be back with the chairman."

Boy I hope we can get this stuff up to the police department or someplace safe. This ordinance should be locked up. That's what I'll suggest to the chairman and the police. Put it in the jail.

Howard, age thirty-eight, an army veteran with experience in Iraq, jogged his out-of-shape figure toward the longhouse.

Jesus.

Chapter 28

Agency Longhouse

Martha had known that she was supposed to be here, that her *kutkut,* her work was to lead with wisdom, the wisdom of her parents, of her dead husband, in order for the people to survive.

She spoke quietly, as she was accustomed to. If people couldn't hear her, they needed to listen better.

"My grandson Gopher, he became a man in the last two days. That is what we all must do, become the people again. He was visiting his *Ala*, when the bad men came to Simnasho. I'm sure you have heard of it. Bad men came from off the reservation and killed and burned houses, and took over our beautiful town. The town of the Wasco's."

She let her voice grow harsh at the end.

"I was born here on the reservation. I know all of you. I will help with the elders to bring the old ways back, to gather and put up food, to raise the children.

Nicole watched and listened to the little Indian woman, a person afflicted with arthritis by the way she walked. She was amazed that a frail older person could command such respect, could get everyone to listen to her.

I want to get to know her, to learn from her.

Nicole knew that she had to get Weasel back to the clinic so he could rest, but he refused. He wanted to stay and she had to admit that she did too. She was so thankful to be here with Weasel and these people, rather than running to survive in L.A. She looked over at Weasel in the darkness by the stage, and suddenly kissed him on the neck. Weasel slowly turned his head, and even in the darkness, she could tell that he was smiling.

"Maybe we should go back to the clinic a little early, while all the people are here. I'm feeling a little tired." He chuckled.

"If you're feeling that good, maybe we should leave now."

Weasel put his good arm around Nicole, and held her close to him as they listened to Martha.

Martha stopped and let the auditorium grow quiet. "I want to talk with you for a minute about my good friend, a good tribal worker, Martin Andrews. He is fearless, and he fights for us. He is a good man, I am proud to call him friend, and we need to rely on him, on his wisdom." She made as if to reach behind her, and Martin came up with Lori.

"Martin, you saved all of us from having to endure the dog suit again." And as Martha said this, the crowd clapped and laughed. Martin waved and took Lori back to their spot beside the podium.

"One more thing." Martha put her hand in her bag. "When we go to take our beloved town back from those evil men, I will be one of the leaders. When two of them chased poor Cecilia, you know Jim Burns's daughter up my driveway to my house, I used my dead husband's revolver and sent them to their maker." And with that,

Martha pulled the huge revolver from her purse and held it down by her side.

"When we go to take our town, our reservation back from those evil men, me and my revolver will be with the Wasco chief, and with police Chief Andrews, and we will be in the front." And with that she waved the heavy revolver above her head, the pain from her arthritis nearly caused her to drop the 44-40 cannon. The noise from the crowd was enormous. They were standing, clapping, yelling.

Martha put the revolver back in her purse, and waited for the noise to subside. When it was quiet again, she started to sing in a quiet voice, a prayer for the people, singing in Sahaptin. Her voice grew stronger, the notes flowing into the microphone, and to someone who hadn't heard her before, her voice was surprisingly beautiful. She finished her prayer, looking over the assembly, and knew that they would survive. Too many good people here to not. She did not believe that she would make it to the end of the fight, but she would show them enough of the old ways to carry them along.

She felt an arm around her, and Bluefeathers was there. He leaned forward to speak.

"I am Wasco too, and will be in the front with Martha Couer d' Alenes, and our Wasco chief. And tonight, all of us, we are all Wasco. We will take back our land."

The audience yelled, with cries of "Kill them!"

Bluefeathers helped Martha off the stage and took her to where her family was waiting. As he started to walk up to the podium, Martin gestured to him. Howard Kewa was bent over, talking to Martin. He appeared agitated. Bluefeathers stepped over to where they were standing.

"Mr. Chairman, you have to hear this. Go ahead, Howard."

The words came out in a rush, and when he told what he had seen, Bluefeathers didn't know if it was good fortune, or a curse to have such things on the reservation. He held his hand up.

"Martin, go with him and take care of it. Maybe take the truck to the corrections center, see if you can off-load it. And Howard, let Martin know right away if you find more military equipment in other trucks. I want a complete inventory of the trucks as soon as you can get it."

Bluefeathers looked at them. Martin nodded, and he and Lori started to follow Howard out of the longhouse. Bluefeathers returned to the podium. He had more to say, more to do this night. He wished his granddaughter Tara were here with him. She had the wisdom of an elder. He couldn't let his worry for her show. She was away in that white man's law school, over there in Eugene. He knew she would survive, and would show her *Šiyápu* friends how to survive with her.

Bluefeathers, the tribal council chairman for the Cold River Indian Reservation of Oregon, a decorated Marine veteran of the Whites war in Vietnam, a former police officer and police chief, suddenly felt very tired, and all of his seventy-six years. But he knew how to fight, and fight they would. He stepped up to the microphone.

Chapter 29

Pelton Dam, Reservation side

Keelah looked out across the Dam to the United States. That's how they referred to the land off the reservation – United States, State of Oregon, Whitey land, or a host of other names. Smokey had told them that they would be getting night vision devices, but he sure as hell hadn't seen them yet. The clouds had moved in, and without starlight or moonlight, it was pure dark. He didn't like working with the police, but for now, he didn't see as if they had any choice. He had been in the tribal jail youth detention for years.

Charles, his second in command, was beside him.

"You see that?"

"No, what?"

"Movement on the top of the dam. A shadow."

Keelah looked harder, wishing again for night vision. He didn't want to give their position away. The 18th Streeters had already shot one of his boys a few days ago, what if it was them coming across the dam? He didn't trust that fuck George as far as he could throw the dam. And the 18th Street assholes seemed to be in the favor of the police. All the more reason to open up. He had his crew spread out every half mile from here to the bridge.

He saw more movement on top of the dam, just down to his right, and he decided to give the order.

"Light up the dam!"

A spotlight came on from above them, and began sweeping the road on top of the dam. The beam passed two figures literally caught like a deer in the headlights, and then swept back and held on them. They began to run back to the other side, when one of Keelah's homies opened up on them with an automatic rifle.

"What the Fuck!" Keelah yelled. "Stop firing, you fuck, who gave the…?"

And he watched as a figure crumpled on the dam. The other one ran back across the top of the dam, running for the far side, limping, and then he went down. He lay there, twitching, flopping in the spotlight. His arm came up like a bird's broken wing, and then he was still.

The light held steady, and the shooter stopped firing.

An SUV pulled up on the road to the dam, lights out, and Keelah knew it was Smokey, and others. He slung his AR and walked up to the road. Smokey stepped out of the passenger side of the SUV, holding a backpack.

"What the fuck, Keelah? I hope they were assaulting you?"

"A little mix-up there, Lieutenant. One of my homies got a little excited."

"Let's see."

Keelah looked closely at the driver, and realized that it was the Chief of Police himself. He stayed seated in the car.

Smokey produced a flashlight and led the way down the road to the dam. A gang member was there to let them in the gate.

As they got to the middle, they all saw what the gang had dropped.

"Shit." Smokey kneeled down and looked at the nearest one. "Aw, shit, Keelah." He stood up and looked at the gang leader. "Take a good look at what your shooter has done. Fuck!" The kid was missing a part of his head, lying in a pool of blood. Smokey walked to the other one. He had wounds in the chest and head, blood leaking out in a pool that was starting to congeal in the cool air. He started back across the dam, turned back, and said, "meet me at the car."

At the car, Keelah stood and waited to hear from Smokey what he had to hear. He wasn't going to take an undue amount of shit from him, but at some level he knew he had to play their game, because if they went to war with the tribes, they eventually would be killed by their own tribal members. Keelah had some respect for the Lieutenant, even if he was a cop, since he had been over there in Afghanistan several times, and had been in some real shit.

"What the hell, they're just kids, maybe twelve years old, not even armed. They're just hungry. What the hell did I say."

Smokey appeared to be trying to control himself.

"Yeah, it won't happen again. My discipline will be swift. We will fix it." He appreciated that the lieutenant hadn't gotten in his face in front of the gang, that would have been bad for all of them.

"We could use some night vision." Keelah said.

Smokey handed over the backpack. “Armed invaders,” Smokey said. “Shoot armed invaders, otherwise, a warning shot. Bring the bodies over here and get rid of them.”

Keelah nodded.

Smokey returned to the SUV and Keelah heard him tell the chief that they needed to meet Lori at the truck and check it out, whatever that meant. He watched as they turned with chirping tires, and then it was gone, a black SUV swallowed up in the night.

At least he had night vision.

Chapter 30

Agency Longhouse

Bluefeathers was tired. He had an internal drive that wouldn't let him quit, and sooner or later it would kill him. *Probably sooner*, he thought. He was an elder, and needed to think of himself as what he was, an *xwsaat,* an old man. He looked over the dark auditorium, and realized that with the different speakers coming and going, some of the people had left. Most were still here though, and he had more to say. He knew that he had to wrap this up to keep them here. He took a deep breath.

I will tell them about Tara, to give them hope. They are getting restless, finish this up, show them how to wat wisa, to lead the way, old man.

"For a long time now, we have said bad things about the *Siyapu*, about their way of treating the Natives. But we have taken their handouts, their money, even with their taking our land."

The room grew quiet.

"Even though the Great White Father in Washington promised us many things in the treaty of 1855, and he promised us that he would take care of the Native people's health, education, and welfare in perpetuity, forever – those things are a treaty right. But we have looked upon that money, that help, in a way a dependent child would, and we have become children. We haven't made too much noise when the Great White Father and his minions have continued to steal our land. Again and again.

"We have become dependent children. And make no mistake, there are whites here who are our friends and we are their friends, as you have heard, some have fought with us. But now, we are a community, all of us here, tribal member and *Siyapu*, we must learn from each other. We will survive."

He said that quietly, and there were murmurs in the crowd.

"My granddaughter, Tara, is in Eugene, going to school. Many of you have loved ones away, and the one thing I know is that they will use their native heritage, their knowledge of the old ways, to help them survive, and the *Siyapu* around them. One thing I know, is that we will now show the *Siyapu* how to survive, without their handouts."

He held his hands up as the applause started. He had a ways to go.

"We have a time to plant, with the elders help, we have a time to gather, we have a time to fish, to hunt, to put food up in the old way for the winter. If this had come in November, we would not survive very well, I think. As most of you know, we have kept a number of trucks that were traveling through the reservation. We will have food banks at the community center and in this building starting in a week. Survive until then, with your own food, neighbors food, and your gathering.

"The police are in charge of security, and Lieutenant Smokey Kukup, Army veteran, is in charge of security for threats from the outside. If you have military experience, please contact Smokey as soon as possible. There are groups who will be a'comin' to take what we have."

A voice came from the audience.

"Let them try!"

Applause started immediately.

"I know, and I feel the same way," Bluefeathers said. "But they may be many. We will make alliances where we can. We will survive."

"What about the truckers, people new to the reservation? Do we kick them off?"

"I want to introduce a couple of people," Bluefeathers said, and he waved to people behind him, standing in the dark.

A group of fifteen men and five women crowded onto the stage behind the chairman. They wore work clothes, some of them shorts and T-shirts. Most had their hands in their pockets, some looking confident, some scared.

"These are the men and women who were driving trucks through the reservation when the electricity stopped. We diverted trucks, as you know. We gave the drivers a choice – stay here, or we will take you to the border. These drivers agreed to stay and help. I want you to meet one of them, Mohammad. I don't know where he is from, but he agreed to stay here. A tall man with a turban approached the microphone.

"Hello, I am Mohammad. I chose to be here to help." His English was on the edge of understandable. He got his point across, Bluefeathers thought.

“I come from India, and my family is in Fairfax, Virginia. I hope and pray they are okay. I want you to know that I am from a tribe, such as yours. I now want to help your tribe. I will swear loyalty to you, you have my life.” And with that, he turned around and walked back to the group. The people sat quietly, and Bluefeathers thought that they didn’t know what to say. He finally spoke.

“Housing will find a way to help those people find houses.” Bluefeathers looked out again, and asked, “Questions?” People were leaving, slipping out quietly, going home to figure out what their families needed.

“Chairman Bluefeathers.” The speaker was an elder, Robert Talfer. “Chairman Bluefeathers, what if we have a need for a certain medicine? Is that little plane going to help us?”

“I don’t know, but if it is possible, we will do it.”

“Chairman!”

The speaker was a man they all knew as “The Colonel”. He had never been in the service as far as Bluefeathers knew, but that was his name, and he was a serious threat to keep the whites off the reservation, no matter what good they did.

“Yes, Colonel.”

“How can we survive if we keep feeding and taking care of those who seek to destroy us at every turn?”

“We will survive, and we will survive with our will and the old ways, but we live in a world where we must judge just how we do that long term. I share your concern, Colonel.”

The meeting was winding down, and he knew he had to close.

"Stay close to your families, keep each other safe, volunteer for the work that needs to be done." He looked off to the east, from where he stood. He paused, and then spoke softly.

"A century and a half ago, The U.S. Calvary camped here, just over there." He waved his arm toward the east wall. "If you look hard, you can see the white tents of the Army, down there along Shitike Creek. General Crook was here. We had a difficult time then, and we have a difficult time now. We must keep our reservation and people alive, and at the same time, not destroy our relationship with the outside world, for it is as it has always been – the numbers of our enemies will overwhelm us. We will find our friends wherever we need to find them, to survive."

He held his right hand up in a benediction as well as a goodbye. Bluefeathers knew that within the next month, their numbers would be fewer, and he might not be around as well.

He couldn't have guessed just how much the world of the Cold River Indian Reservation would change, and when he thought about it later, he was glad that he didn't know on this day.

And the change was deadly, and happening as he left the podium.

The Cold River Indian Reservation of Oregon was about to be under assault from all sides. From the forests, from the highways, from the river, and from the lakes.

People who were starving held the thought that there was a lot of food on the reservation, and there were a lot of them, and they had guns.

They were coming.

DAY THREE

"We are not at war with our neighbors. We are in a war of survival. We will help our true friends, as they will help us. Now, in these days after the electricity is gone, we have only friends or enemies."

- Chairman Bluefeathers

Chapter 30

D&D Garage, temporary hanger

Nicole hugged herself, trying to stay warm. She was a southern California girl, and wasn't used to the cold mornings of the high desert. The temperature was in the high thirties, and the sun was just coming up. They were in the D&D Garage, an auto repair shop, just down from the Community Center and a block from the longhouse. This was the building the police decided the plane should be kept. The garage made a secure hanger and was under twenty-four-hour-guard. The people in charge took the value of the plane as seriously as they did the guarding of food.

Nicole watched as Weasel walked around the Cessna. He had insisted on going to the hanger to inspect his plane, and she and Doctor Semington had accompanied him. He wore his arm in a sling, and Nicole was worried that he would do too much too soon and open up the wound. She knew that gunshot wounds took a long time to heal, that they had to heal from the inside, and looked ugly for weeks. This had been just days, and Weasel was pretending that he was okay.

Semington stood by the door, watching his patient.

"Plane looks good," Weasel said. "You didn't crash it, or bounce it." He said this as if it were a surprise, and when he came around the side to check the tail gear, Nicole nudged him.

"I made a landing with no help from you, you were snoozing. And it didn't bounce, there are a lot of witnesses to the perfect landing I made."

He laughed, and she surprised herself by laughing with him. He ran his hands over the metal skin of the plane like a lover touching his woman. Nicole turned around and caught him looking at her jeans.

"You want to touch that again," she said, "You might want to say nice things about my flying ability." He laughed and started for the left side door when they were joined by Smokey.

"Can you fly this today?" Smokey asked. He was wearing a rumpled tribal police uniform, and looked as if he hadn't slept in the three days since the electricity had gone off.

"I can." He winced as he slowly moved around the plane, holding his arm. Semington moved from the doorway to join the discussion. Smokey looked at the inscription on the pilot's door.

"Nice touch, Weasel. Nice."

"Well, in L.A. it was a little different. But the last time I flew for the Rez, for Bluefeathers, I thought this was fitting. What's up, Lieutenant?"

"We need to know what is going on around the reservation, from the roads in the north, to Simnasho, and the border here along the river. Maybe even take a short run over Madras to see what's happening there and get an idea of what we're facing."

"We can do that," Weasel said, "But we are going to need some 110 octane. We don't want to start off with what we put into the tanks in Fort Rock."

"We have some on its way. They had some at Federal Fire Management for the helicopters that often land there. The rest is under guard."

Nicole looked closely at Weasel. She knew him well enough by now to know that there was not much that would keep him from flying today, unless the Doctor stepped in hard, and even that might not help. Weasel said that he felt okay, so here he was.

While the plane was being fueled under Weasel's supervision, Nicole and Smokey and Semington had a conference. They stood and watched the pilot as he carefully made his way around the plane.

"He really okay to fly?" Smokey asked.

"Depends," Semington said. "This is not a new activity for him, so he should be okay. Depends on how much pain-killer he has in his system, for starters. If he were going up alone, I would take the keys from him. But with Nicole, she'll know if he's acting loopy, and she can land the plane. I would give him a cautious thumbs up. I want to know what's out there as much as anyone."

Nicole watched Weasel as he waited for the tanks to be filled.

He's torn between taking care of the plane, and finding out what we're talking about. She waved and blew him a kiss, trying to reassure him and knowing that he would just have to deal with it.

"He says he hasn't taken any pain-killers today, none since last night, and I don't think he has," Nicole told them.

"I think it will be okay. For flights, Nicole, watch his medication. We need him, you, and this plane," Semington said. "Check with me when you get back and we'll look at his wound."

As the doctor walked away, Smokey pulled a duffle bag from his Tahoe. He walked over to the plane with Nicole, and put it on the ground by the passenger door.

"Food, water, shotgun, extra ammo for your Glock."

Nicole nodded. She knew that if they were forced to land at anyplace other than back here, they would need the gear. "I have a first aid and field surgical kit in my bag," she said. Smokey handed her a radio.

"Trade me your radio, this was fully charged last night."

"Thanks, Lieutenant. We'll be okay."

"We're good to go," Weasel said. "Let's push the plane out and we'll taxi to the road. Smokey, can you lead the way with your car when we get started?"

They pushed the Cessna out and found that they had an audience. There was a group of people standing in the parking lot, watching, talking.

"Weasel!"

Sammy Standing Bear came from the crowd. Weasel waved him over.

"Can you fly over my family's house up there on the B200 road, you know, where the old logging camp was?"

"We will be over that way, along the tree line. I'll let you know."

"Thanks, Weasel. Glad you're here." He looked at Nicole and gave her a knowing smile, and walked back to the crowd.

Oh Lordy, when is this ever going to stop. Well, I guess I might as well smile about it, considering that Weasel and I made it official last night in his room in the clinic. I am his woman.

She smiled and got in the passenger side. Weasel went through the preflight from the cockpit, and started the Lycoming engine. Nicole felt a thrill as the engine came to life, and even with the horrible anarchy the country was going through, she was going on an adventure like none other. She thanked the Creator (as Weasel called God) every hour that she was in the right place to take this journey with him. Her affection for him was growing with each hour, and she was pleasantly surprised to find Weasel to be a tender and caring lover.

They followed Smokey's black Tahoe down Hollywood street. Nicole waved as they passed the community center. People were on the sidewalk, waving, smiling.

Smokey blocked the road at the highway, and Weasel powered up the engine and touched Nicole's hand. He released the brakes and the Cessna shot forward. They were airborne in seconds. Nicole felt a flush through her body. She looked to the left as they flew over the Casino and then the lumber mill. They were now over the Deschutes River and Weasel banked to the right, gaining altitude. They had decided to not go off the reservation until the end of their flight, and would do so at a much higher altitude. If something happened when they were over Madras at eight thousand feet, they could conceivably glide back to the reservation.

They flew over Cold River and Nicole got a look at the layout of the town.

They flew up the highway with Mt. Jefferson towering to their left and Mt. Hood straight ahead just thirty miles away.

They flew north toward Mt. Hood along the tree line, and Nicole saw houses, some in clusters, and others more secluded. There was smoke ahead.

"Weasel, look." She pointed.

"I see it, we'll fly over." He turned the plane toward the smoke. As they got closer, Weasel put the flaps down and slowed the plane. He pointed. "That's the Johnson place. Looks like the house and barn burned."

The house was in a clearing in the trees, and as they got to the edge of the clearing, Nicole saw two bodies on the ground in front of the house. She looked with her binoculars. "A man and a woman, I think," she said.

"Take command," Weasel told Nicole. Before she had a chance to say anything, he reached for the binoculars. "Keep our speed and altitude the same, and come around so I can get a look."

Weasel looked as she turned, and he grimly handed her the binoculars. "My airplane," he said. His face was drawn, and Nicole thought his color was bad.

Why the hell didn't I see that when we were in the hanger? You know why, Nicole old kid, you wanted to go up and see what was happening as much as Weasel. Dammit Nicole!

"Hey, Babe, you okay?" Weasel nodded. He put his hand on her shoulder and then retracted the flaps, increasing power. They were in a climb back to the north.

"Make an entry in your notebook of the time and place. Johnson place on fire, two bodies in front of the house, I believe to be Horse Johnson and his wife Sheryl."

"Were they friends of yours, Weasel?"

He nodded and they flew northeast, toward the Mt. Hood Highway. Smokey wanted to know what the road to the north looked like between Government Camp and the upper boundary of the Rez. They flew near the northern boundary. There was a blockade there, and a camp. Weasel wagged the wings, and a figure in the group waved. They had a fire going in their encampment.

"Look at that," Weasel said. He drifted over the trees just off the highway to their left. "That's the he-he longhouse."

"Who are those people?"

There were a large number of cars, trailers, and motor homes in the parking lot. "People who made it over the pass from Portland, I expect."

"Like the gang in Simnasho?"

"I don't think so. Looks like people who left Portland and made it this far. Just note that and Smokey will have to deal with it later."

As they came up over the pass Mt. Hood towered over them on the right. The radio on Nicole's hip crackled.

"Multnomah County Corrections, anybody copy?"

The voice was strained, almost frantic, which was unusual for a law enforcement dispatcher. They were usually cool. Nicole decided to answer.

"We copy. Mt Hood area."

"Are you Law Enforcement?"

"Yes, Cold River."

"As in the Reservation?"

"Yes."

"Shit. We need help here, all the deputies who left on calls haven't returned, and the same for Portland Police Bureau. Some of us from both agencies are on the upper floors of the justice center, have no help anywhere."

"Can you go outside?" Nicole could only imagine. The response clarified that for her.

"No, to go outside, even in force, we would last a half block. Whole sections of the town are on fire, bodies everywhere. The bridges are blocked. Interstate 5 and I-205 are filled with burned out cars."

"Tell them to stay there, find some food and water," Weasel said. "That's all we can do."

"County," Nicole said, "We think the only thing you can do is to stay put. Sorry."

They gained altitude and passed the northern boundary. They had been flying over a solid forest for that last fifteen miles, and they watched the road in silence. There were cars, trucks, RV's strung along the road, a fair number of them burned out. In one place just south of the ski area at Government Camp, a large number of cars and trucks were jumbled up and on fire.

Nicole put the binoculars up and was at once sorry she did. In the wreckage there were bodies, some burned, grotesque shapes of what had been human, with loved ones, hopes, jobs, dreams. Her mouth went dry when the powerful binoculars came upon a small figure with her arm outstretched, a doll flung out from a hand, forgotten and alone. She felt her emotions get the best of her and tears flooded the eyepieces. She pulled the glasses down and wiped her face.

There were campfires and groups of people stranded on the sides of the roads. Families. Children.

"Can we turn around now," she said, her voice cracking. "I want to go back."

As Weasel turned the plane and headed back to the reservation land, he finally spoke.

"It's one thing to imagine it, another to see it."

"Yeah," Nicole said. She felt hollow, and knew she sounded the same way. What scared her, and Weasel she was sure, was that this scene below them was being played out all across the country. She wanted to cry again, but knew she couldn't now. She wanted nothing more than for her man to hold her, and not have to be the big tough nurse and cop she presented to everyone. She just wanted to be held.

"Those people down there, they're not going to make it are they?"

Weasel waited to answer, and Nicole knew that he needed some time. When he finally spoke, his voice was soft.

"Most likely not, *Atauwit.*"

"'What's that word, *Atauwit?"*

Weasel looked out the windscreen, and said, "loved one."

Nicole leaned over and kissed his neck. She didn't know what else to do.

As last Weasel said, "Please make an entry of what we saw up there."

Her hand trembled as she wrote.

Their radio came to life as they neared the Simnasho junction.

"Weasel, this is Smokey. You there?"

"Nicole here, yes we are."

"If you haven't already, fly over the three areas we talked about, the blocking areas. George is requesting contact at the south one."

"Roger that," Nicole said. "We are close to the west and north ones, will make notes, and then head to the south one."

"Copy, be careful over the town."

Weasel turned back to the west and circled, gaining altitude. It wouldn't do to fly over Simnasho and get shot down. He wanted at least five thousand feet AGL. They flew over the blockade to the west of Simnasho and saw figures, hoping they were part of the 18th Street group. At the north road, three miles from Simnasho, the blockade had been set up in a road cut. The cars had been moved and there were bodies on the ground. Nicole wrote as they flew over toward Simnasho.

She wrote: *Simnasho, several houses burned, with bodies on the ground. A large number of cars, pickups, motorcycles around the longhouse and fire station. There were people, most with rifles in front of the fire station. Three Warriors Market burned.*

People were looking up and pointing. They flew over at an idle, quiet, but they were spotted anyway. Rifles fired, and by that time they were a mile high, and moving south. They flew over the southern blockade and the people down there were waving.

"Weasel." Smokey came on the radio.

"Passing over the south," Nicole said.

"Can you land there?"

"Let me check."

Weasel slowed the plane, Nicole was on the glasses.

"I will let down and land on the road to the south of the roadblock."

"Weasel." A new voice came over the radio.

"Air Cold River, go ahead," Nicole said. Weasel squeezed her leg, attention outside, flying the plane.

"If you can land, we need to talk. This is George Wolfhead."

Weasel was turning around above the Kah Nee Ta Resort, now mostly deserted. There was a housing area there for workers, and they saw some activity there. Nicole recorded this as they slowed and came back from the south, flying over Indian Head Canyon.

"On our way," Nicole said.

The landing was smooth, a quarter mile south of the blockade. As they taxied they were approached by three armed people.

"That's George," Weasel said. Nicole watched as a large man with tattoos on his head and arms approached. The rifle looked small in his hands. Weasel turned the engine off and the prop came to a stop. He opened his door and waited, keeping his seatbelt and harness fastened. The gang leader had what looked like blood smeared on his forehead, face and arms. Finger painting.

"Hey, Weasel," George said, shaking Weasel's hand. He peered into the cabin and smiled. "Hi, I heard Weasel had a woman."

Aw, for chrissakes. Does everyone know, even up here?

"That would be me. Nicole."

"George, before we talk, can you and your men turn the plane around. I want to be pointed back south in case something happens."

George gave the order and they waited while the plane was turned.

"Tell Smokey we need more people and ammunition for 12 gauge and AR's. We knocked them back, but they will hit us again, they know where we are."

Nicole wrote and listened.

"Uh, George, your northern blockade is down. Bodies on the road."

"Son-of-a-bitch!" George said. "We thought they might be gone, but now we know for sure. Those assholes in Simnasho can now get off the reservation and get more people and supplies. Chief Martin and Smokey give me enough people we'll take them out like rats in a barrel. I just need the word. They're dead men up there, and the sooner the better."

George handed Weasel a folded paper. "What we need, and a summary of our action, for Smokey, and for tribal notes."

"George, I have to ask," Nicole said, "What's with the blood?"

He looked closely at her. "Blood of our enemies." He pointed to a young girl, his woman apparently. She held a shotgun and a fierce smile. She had a small amount of blood on her forehead, dainty almost. Well, after all, she was a woman.

"You will know our enemies by their blood on our bodies," George said. "Before this is over, we will be well painted, I think."

Nicole had a wild thought. *You folks ever hear of bloodborne pathogens, but I guess at this point, it doesn't matter.*

She had to stifle a laugh, just the same.

"Nice to meet you, George," Nicole said.

George replied in Spanish. "Very nice to meet you, you dark-haired beauty, ever get tired of the pilot, let me know." He laughed, and shook Weasel's hand, winked at Nicole. "You be safe, my Amigo."

He saluted them and stood back as Weasel started the engine.

The take off was quick, and then they were over the canyon.

"I caught some of that, what was that about, the Spanish?"

Nicole told him, and added, "I do not believe he was being disrespectful to you, I think he meant it in a good way, as a compliment to you, Weasel my gorgeous lover."

Weasel nodded, and that seemed to satisfy him, but you never could tell with a man.

They flew over Wolf point, Weasel pointing out places as Nicole wrote. Sunnyside looked pretty normal, Weasel said, and in each place, people waved.

"Madras, then home," Weasel said, climbing. They flew across the river, and up the canyon toward Madras, a town with a population of ten thousand, ten miles from the reservation.

"I didn't see a gang leader back there," Nicole said softly. "I didn't see a gangbanger, even with all of his gang and prison tats. I saw instead a warrior, a tribal leader, who is now thinking about tribal history and his place in it, maybe for the first time in his life."

"Maybe you're right," Weasel said. "He's not very old, but he seems older, maybe wiser that I have ever thought of him before." He sat for a minute, and then said, "Let's tell Martin and Smokey that. It's information they can use. I have a feeling that we are going to need every warrior, every leader we can find."

They saw the smoke from the fires in Madras as soon as they flew above the river.

Weasel approached Madras from the north. They flew over the airport with it's two-mile runway, keeping high to avoid rifle fire.

The World War II museum had been partially burned. There were six fire fighting air tankers out front. Two of the large jets smoldered.

They came over the airport from the Northeast. Weasel turned to the west and slowed the aircraft. Nicole looked at him. Under any other circumstances, it would have been a beautiful flight. From where they were, they were close to Mt. Bachelor ski area, Mt. Washington, the Three Sisters Mountains, Broken Top, Mt. Jefferson on the reservation, and Mt. Hood, all of them snow covered, with a carpet of forest leading up to the peaks.

The sun was well up to the east.

"What are we doing?"

"I want to make a low pass, fast, you look and take notes. Highway 97 and Highway 26 come together on the north end of town, and on the south end, Hwy 126 takes off to the south east. The town is about four miles long, spread out along the highways."

"You think that's a good plan, my sweetheart?"

"Well, we were shot at in Simnasho at a mile high. They had time to see us. Let's just buzz the town, fast, at two hundred feet, they won't be able to react in time to get a shot off and we'll be gone. When we get to the south, we'll circle to the west, and get some altitude. The airport looks compromised."

"Okay. Let's do it."

Weasel put the Cessna into a dive, and when they leveled off they shot over Safeway (burning) and the Les Schwab Tire store. Nicole knew that the world was falling apart, but what a rush! Flashing over buildings, burning cars, bodies in the street, the sun as bright as ever, the surreal scene was out of a Hollywood apocalypse movie, only this was real. They came up on the Thriftway Grocery, and saw a roadblock that stretched across three blocks. Cars, trucks, even a school bus, blocking the one-way highways going north and south in the middle of town.

A lone car moved south of the roadblock. Glass from the windows of the Bi Mart drug and grocery store littered the parking lot like the glitter of dirty diamonds. The TS&S Ford dealership was on fire as were most of the cars in the lot. Welcome to Madras, Mr. Thomas.

The Chevy dealership was mostly intact, surrounded by old cars and guards. People were moving, pointing, and then they were past, and Weasel was banking and climbing to the west and back around the town. They were out of sight of the dealership with the people. Nicole scribbled in her journal. The roads south of Madras were blocked.

There were bodies everywhere.

They were climbing as they approached the airport from the south, when the radio in Nicole's lap startled them.

"Cessna over Madras, this is Jimmy Asher. Do you copy me?'

Nicole looked at Weasel.

"The County Sheriff. Jimmy." Weasel slowed on the west side of the airport and leveled off. No houses down below, they were over Willow Creek Canyon. They could see the airport from here, two miles east.

Nicole picked up the radio and held her hands up to Weasel. She didn't know what to say. He gave her a thumbs up, and she spoke.

"This is Cold River Air."

Weasel laughed.

"Uh, yeah, is that you, Weasel?"

Nicole handed the radio to Weasel. "Yes, Jimmy, I flew up here from L.A. when the power went out."

"Be advised, this is not a secure channel. I need a meet with Bluefeathers, Chief Andrews, Smokey, you, others. Soon. We got a situation here, and we should work together to survive."

"Well, we all got a situation. I will tell them, Jimmy. Is it safe to land?" The sheriff's office and corrections compound was a hundred yards from the airport.

"No, we have tried to keep the hangers clear, lost some good men and women trying in the last two days. We can clear it in the day, marauders take it back again in the night. Can't land, Weasel. Sorry."

Weasel flew on toward the reservation, a three-minute flight. He kept altitude to be able to talk with the sheriff.

"How many people you got there?"

"About two hundred, we can keep the compound and jail and offices safe, but to venture outside is sporty. We need stuff." Nicole came back on the radio.

"Sheriff, this is Nicole. We saw a roadblock stretching across Madras at about the Thriftway store, to the dealerships. What's up with that?"

"A group of survivors, and a slaughtering group, is taking whatever and whomever they find, killing and taking. They are getting stronger."

"Weasel says we will report to Bluefeathers and Chief Martin Andrews. How can we contact you?"

"Have your dispatch monitor the county emergency frequency each hour. We will call them."

"Okay, will do. Bye for now."

"Nicole?"

"Yes, Sheriff."

"Nice to meet Weasel's woman."

She dropped the radio in her lap, and shoved Weasel's good shoulder. He was grinning as he put the flaps down for a straight in approach past the mill and up the road to the turn.

"Oh for the love of it, Weasel, how the hell does everyone, on and off the Rez, know about us, even before I did? WTF, Weasel, in this short of a time period, how does this happen?"

The wheels touched down from their incredible journey, and Weasel said, "In-din time, Short Stuff. In-din time, my beautiful woman." He laughed and pulled her to him as they taxied up the hill. Nicole joined him, trying to push away the utter destruction and death of their world that she had seen today. They laughed, and touched each other, arms, hands, faces. They were alive for now.

They wouldn't laugh again for a long time.

Chapter 31

D&D Garage

Martha Couer d'Alenes watched as the airplane with the wing on top came slowly down the road and past the community center and rodeo grounds where the trucks were parked. She had been told to wait for the woman, Nicole. The Police Chief Martin Andrews had asked Martha if she could bring Nicole to him.

Martha stood in the shadow of the awning and waited. *At least my arthritis that is eating up my bones is at rest, thank you, Lord. I can see Weasel and Nicole there in the plane. I am going to wave if my arthritis doesn't act up too much, but Lordy after shooting the revolver, it sure has been aching. That Weasel, who had run off to fly big planes, was waving as if he were a fool. At least he is back now where he belongs. And he brought this nice woman with him.*

Nicole reached up and shut the engine off and the three-bladed prop came to a stop.

"So, how'd I do taxiing, my instructor?"

"You're getting a handle on moving around on the road," Weasel said, and winced. Nicole had been worried about him since they had left the ground on this surveillance flight. His normal almond-colored skin was grey, and every little movement brought a wince of pain from him. She had no doubt that he was putting on a brave face for her and Doctor Semington, but she knew wounds and how long they took to heal.

"Let's get the plane in the garage, and to bed with you, rest and some drugs."

Weasel nodded, and she thought that for once, he was too tired and in too much pain to argue. Nicole got out and walked around to help Weasel out. They had a small group of watchers at the hanger. They would have help getting the plane rolled in.

"Nicole."

Martha called to her. Nicole walked over and greeted her.

"Hi, Martha."

"The police need you to come to a house with me," Martha said. "We have a ride."

"Martha, can we take Weasel to the clinic on the way? He needs to be back in bed."

"Before the clinic, we had the old ways, but Weasel needs this new medicine, living down there in California all this time."

It didn't sound like a bad thing to Nicole, just a matter-of-fact statement from the elder. Once the plane was secure, Nicole helped Weasel into the car.

"I wonder what that old woman wants?" Weasel asked as Nicole walked him into the clinic and eased him into a chair.

Nicole shrugged. "I like her."

"Oh, I'm not suggesting you can refuse her," Weasel said. "If she is asking for you, just go with it." He slumped in the chair. Nicole caught Semington's eye as he came out of the ER, in scrubs, bloody gloves. He rushed over, a man in a hurry.

"I have to get right back in there." He looked at Weasel. "Maybe some pain meds now?" Semington looked closer at his patient. "Bed for him, the rest of the day."

"I agree," Nicole said, and kissed Weasel on his forehead. "I have my notes, will report to the chief," she said, looked at the doctor, and walked out.

Back in the car, Martha turned to her. "We only have a short distance, a house about a half mile from town. The chief asked for me to find you, he asked for you."

"Why me?"

"Because of your skill as a nurse, a cop. He needs your evaluation of a situation."

"Oh."

"I had a feeling about you when I first heard that you landed the plane on the road. Only Weasel has done that before. I know you were sent here to bring Weasel and the plane. Without you he wouldn't have made it, and we need him, you, and the plane. I believe the Creator sent you to him to take care of him, to be strong for him. He has lived for too long with the whites, he has adopted their ways.

"Someone told me your name is Hernandez. You are also from an In-din tribe in southern Mexico. You are one of us."

"But how did…?"

"I know things, and I am not wrong. You are one of us."

Nicole sat back and thought about what she had just heard. Her dad was from Mexico, and became an American citizen forty years ago. He was very proud of that, and talked about it until he passed away a decade ago. But he had never spoken about any tribal affiliation, although she thought about it from time to time. But how could Martha know?

"Comin' up on the Walking Horse place," their driver said. The house sat back from the road about a hundred yards, with a pasture in front. A small, one-story ranch style house. There were four tribal police cars parked around the drive.

"Martha, what is this?"

"Martin came around and said that some people had died here, that he thought they had been murdered. He wants us to look."

The car stopped behind a black police Tahoe. Nicole stayed where she was.

"Why us, Martha? I'm new here, and they have a lot more police experience than I do. And why you?"

"Me, because I'm an elder, and I know the tribes. They have something there for me, I think. You, the chief said, because Doctor Semington is busy, the medical examiner is in Madras, he won't be comin' around here, and you know how that goes, and you are the only one with medical training they know right now. You have been appointed coroner."

Chief Martin Andrews left the house and started their way. Nicole got out and went around to open Martha's door for her. They stood by the car as Martin approached.

Nicole felt as if she were in a dream, as if the trip from L.A., the shooting, the flight around looking at all the killing, and now to be in a police force for a couple of days. With the world going to hell it was all just too strange.

What the hell am I doing here? Why am I surviving and all the people in cities facing total destruction. Why do they like me, want to include me? Do I remind them subconsciously of what they have lost?

As Martin came up to them, she had another thought.

Don't knock it, kid. As you told Weasel, your cat ran off two months ago, and you would be holed up in your apartment listening to the world crash, wondering how long your food and water would hold out. The chief looks real bad, oh God, I hope I look better than he does. Has he even slept since this started?

He started without preamble. "Martha, Nicole, there's a bad scene in there. The entire Walking Horse family – Joe, Leslie, and their two children have been murdered. Martha, if you are up to it, I would like for you to come in and tell us for sure who we have, and if this killing is in any way a ritual killing. There are things in there that suggest it is tribal, not from the outside."

He looked to Nicole. "When you look, I want to know, without an autopsy, what killed them. We are through with our part of the crime scene - we will help you examine bodies."

Why me? And then she said, "what if I'm not up to it Chief?"

He gave her a look that she thought was one of exhaustion, and Martin said in a voice that was more weary than unkind, "As long as you wear that uniform, you're up to it."

Instead of taking offense to his words, she was somehow comforted, she was included, and she had been around doctors who were far more abrupt than that. She knew Martin was tired, and watched as he walked the elder woman to the house. They were met on the front porch by an officer who helped Martha put on a pair of booties, the kind worn in an operating room.

Why are they doing this? I understand the need to keep forensic evidence untainted, but has anyone here been keeping score with what is happening in the outside world? We are about to be visited by an army of the apocalypse. What the hell difference does it make. Oh, great, now you're sounding like a politician.

Nicole shook her head and found that she had an appreciation for a chief of police (she had heard that he had been a homicide detective up there in Portland) who still wanted to do things by the book, and she thought that if the electricity came back on, he would not forget this case.

Martin waved to Nicole as he and Martha came out of the house. Martha didn't say anything, but gave Nicole a strange look as they passed in the driveway. It wasn't the look that Martha gave her, it was the booties. The coverings were soaked in what appeared to be blood, up to the top of her feet. The elder left faint red tracks in the gravel of the driveway.

Dear God. Ghost blood tracks from the dead. Stop it.

Nicole put on the booties, her mind steeling itself against what she was going to see, and stood in the doorway. The smell hit her, an overwhelming odor of blood, rot, and feces. The swarm of flies was the worst. Martin pointed at the entryway. It was hard to miss. A medium-sized dog, or what was left of it, was spread out on the linoleum, blood caked on the step. The dog had been eviscerated, its entrails streaming away from the body like a molten flow of bloody lava, thick and dangerous.

"The family's inside," he said, his voice hoarse, a whisper of weariness of a life spent seeing too much death. He leaned outside and took a deep breath, and then stood beside Nicole.

"I'm going to talk about this, Chief, so I don't have to think about it. If you want to record it, fine. Have someone write it anyway, I don't want to have to write it later."

Martin nodded. Nicole started with her narrative.

There's a brown dog in the entryway, disemboweled, the intestines going backward, the dog had tangled up in them before it died. Uh, over in the middle of the room there is what appears to be a woman, with a lot of blood, looks like the same fate as the dog. On the couch, a man, can't tell how old, he has been cut like the dog. I'm going to get more clinical now. I can see from a distance of two feet above the woman that the cuts are from a sharp instrument, surgical, no tearing. There are defensive wounds on the woman, she was cut while she was still alive, with the amount of blood.

Nicole went from the woman to the man, looking, noting what looked to be a gunshot wound in the man's upper chest.

No gun was visible. Huh? The chief said that they didn't find a gun, initially ruling out murder by the man of the wife and kids, then suicide. His wounds were post mortem, anyway, with the significantly smaller amount of blood after he had been shot. There is a door in the corner of the living room, and that's where I don't want to go, but I have to.

The children are on a bed, the master bedroom, stay clinical, and they had been killed. There was blood, oh dear God, the little one killed as well. She had pig-tails, and a green dress, about eight. But they were not eviscerated, they were stabbed, and I have to get out of here. The little girl was on top of her brother, who was maybe ten years old, just thrown there in a parody of sex but thrown there just the same. Who would do this?

Martin is calling me from the kitchen, and I don't need to be here in this room. Cross the living room, you've seen enough, keep your mouth closed against the flies, and just don't breathe.

In the kitchen, the number "88" was finger painted in blood on the refrigerator door. Fucking 88. I need to get out of here. I point at the door and Martin says yes.

Outside, I lean against the wall and take deep breaths, breathing without worrying about flies or ingesting dead flesh, breathing dead flesh into your lungs, for odor is particulate, you see.

Martin came out and leaned against the wall with Nicole.

“What did I see in there? Who would do this, Chief, as if we don’t have enough to worry about.”

“Well, the number 88 suggests that this was done by followers of Adolf Hitler. H is the eighth letter of the alphabet, as in Heil Hitler. I don’t get it, here, in this community. I think this is someone trying to throw us off, but we don’t know that now. There is something wrong with that.”

Nicole blew out her cheeks, and looked at Martin. “What’s wrong with that? What do you think?”

“This isn’t their kind of work. As big of assholes as they might be, they usually just shoot their enemies and get rid of them. This is something else, someone liked this, and tried to make it look like a prison gang was responsible, and the timing is wrong. What do you make of the scene?”

“The dad died first, then the kids. The mom has way too many defensive wounds in her hands and arms, as if she was trying to get person or persons off the kids, and then she was worked on. The dad was worked on after he was killed, the blood is post-mortem after the heart stopped pumping.”

Martin nodded.

“You used to work homicide.” Nicole said it as a statement.

“Yes.”

"Then why do you need me here, why did I have to see that?"

"I wanted someone from the medical profession here. Other than photos, we aren't going to collect and preserve evidence. No time or ability, since we are trying to survive day to day. But make no mistake, we will find out who did this."

Nicole turned to the chief. "I believe you will. So, now we have to worry about who is in our midst, as well as the outside threats."

"It looks that way," Martin said.

"Question?" Nicole said. "Is this a one-time thing, a mass murder, or is this a part of a pattern, going to be a series?"

"Unfortunately, I don't see this as stopping, someone enjoyed hurting people with a knife. We need to find this person."

Martin stood up away from the wall of the house. "Correction, I need to find this person, Smokey and the others are busy."

Nicole put her hand on his arm. "No, you were right, Chief. *We* need to find this person, or persons. We." Martin looked closely at Nicole, and then nodded.

"Thanks."

Nicole pulled off her booties, now looking like the ones Martha had been wearing, and walked slowly back to the car.

I guess you are in this for the duration, kiddo, but damn, why does it have to be so fucked up. Well, you've seen worse as a nurse, so buck up, put on your big girl panties and suck it up.

When she got to the car, Martha reached for her, and she let herself be pulled into an embrace, leaning over the slight elder. Martha held her and whispered, saying words in Sahaptin that Nicole didn't understand, but they were soft and caring, and Nicole began to cry. When she had no more tears, Martha patted her back, whispering to her. She straightened, and gave her a sad smile.

Martha gave her a grim smile in return, patted her arm, and said, "you'll do." Nicole felt as if the little old Indian woman was looking into her soul. They held eye contact for several more seconds, as a mother and daughter, friends who cared for one another. She didn't feel alone anymore.

They rode back to the clinic and Nicole went in to check on her pilot, wanting for the day to be over.

The chief found her in the clinic, sitting by Weasel's bed. The pilot had taken some pain meds, and he was out. Nicole looked up as he came in.

"I am sorry that you had to see that, but we need all the help we can get. When you get time, would you write up what you saw? I know you said you didn't want to, but I don't have anyone else."

"Of course." Nicole got up and stretched. She needed a shower if there was such a thing. She had been dozing with Weasel. "Oh, I want to tell you what we saw on the flight." She took out her notebook, and briefed the chief on what they had observed. He nodded when she told him about George Wolfhead.

"He could be the one to lead the northern forces," Martin said. "Smokey will oversee all of the militia. He will want to know that about George. You just never know who might step up in a crisis."

Nicole told him about Madras, and the threat from the south.

"That's the one we need to worry about, they are eleven miles away. And they could get reinforcements from Redmond, twenty miles south of Madras, Bend, thirty-five miles away. The highway to Portland is probably shut down at several points."

The chief left, and Nicole went to see Semington about a shower. Even if it was a cold one.

Chapter 32

Cold River Tribal Correctional facility

The day room was filled from wall-to-wall and to the ceiling with pallets of green containers. Lieutenant Smokey Kukup leaned on the wall to the kitchen and looked over the assortment of equipment they had removed from the truck. Sergeant Lamebull walked over and leaned against the wall with him. Smokey wanted more than anything to take a nap. He walked to the nearest box.

"We thought that the stuff about Jade Helm was bullshit, L.T., but maybe not."

Smokey agreed. "Well, I don't know what this means, but maybe the conspiracy theories right." He ran his hand over the stenciling.

JADE HELM 2016

And below that was an address

North Pima Rd. Scottsdale, AZ 85251 (WALMART SUPERSTORE)

Smokey knew what his sergeant was talking about, hell they all did. The joint armed forces command had issued orders for a military exercise in the southwest United States, the first ever to combine forces in the interior of the country. The conspiracy theories ran amuck. According to the theory, the military positioned material and personnel in closed Walmart stores in the southwest in preparation for martial law, by order of the president.

Now, as they looked at prepackaged rocket launchers and rifles, complete with munitions, Smokey was not so sure the Jade Helm rumors were a conspiracy. He was still a member of the Army Reserves, and had not paid much attention to the rumors. He had served three tours in Afghanistan, and knew the Army as well as anyone. He had used these weapons, and could teach the use of the rockets in just minutes to almost anyone. It was a gift, and they may well owe their survival to this find.

The other stencil on the pallet containers was "AT4."

A shoulder-fired single-use rocket launcher, with the rocket prepackaged. You put it on your shoulder like a rifle, aim like you would a rifle, hold the safety down, and squeeze. One of the most common light anti-tank weapons in use today. It was a recoilless rifle, with no more kick than a rifle. A kid could fire it.

"How many?" Lamebull asked.

"We don't have a complete inventory yet," Smokey said, "But it looks as if we have over five hundred AT4's and at least a thousand M4 rifles. Enough for a serious defense of this country. And we haven't gone through all of the trucks yet." He looked at the door to the police admin, and saw the chairman and two others come into the jail.

"Boss is here," he announced, and went to greet Chairman Bluefeathers.

Bluefeathers walked up and peered at the cases. He walked around them as Smokey looked on. "Put these with your men at the bridge and along the river, you think, Lieutenant?"

"That's what we had in mind, Mr. Chairman," Smokey said. "Our tribal police personnel and a few military trained people only for now."

Bluefeathers nodded. He looked out the window to the basketball court, and Smokey thought he was thinking of another time.

"We had the M72 LAW in Vietnam," he said. "It was lighter than this, and this little In-din could carry two of them if he had to." He didn't say anything for a minute, staring. He shook his head as if to bring himself back to the present, and then walked down the line to the boxes of M4's. "These are much better than the first M16's we had back then, but they made them better, and we got used to them. The first bunch shipped to Nam got a lot of us Marines killed."

He walked through the room and into the holding cell area, nodding at the cells stacked with boxes.

"MRE's Mr. Chairman. Meals Ready to Eat. We called them the three lies."

Bluefeathers snorted. "You ever had C-rats?" Smokey laughed. He knew Bluefeathers meant C-rations, an older form of food for grunts.

"Sometimes I get a smell of something, and I am back there in 'Nam, eating Charlie Rats. I still can't see the word Turkey, without seeing the box labeled 'Turkey Loaf.' Who the hell would eat something like that?" He laughed.

"Well, I'm sure these are not an improvement, but at least we have cases of them. They will keep you alive, so I've heard."

The chairman gave him a long look and smiled. He drew closer to Smokey. "Your defense will mean our survival. When you get a chance, have one of your men drop off some of the M4's with loaded 30-round magazines to my office. I haven't forgotten how to shoot. Whether it's VC or the invaders across the river, won't make much difference to this old man. Judge Wewana was in the White Man's war in 'Nam with me, he can use one as well." Bluefeathers nodded, looked around again, and left with his assistants.

He must be as exhausted as I am, but he's still in the fight. And he never ceases to amaze me.

Smokey spent the rest of the day in meetings. He went on to organize the trucks. It was decided that they would make four truck parking areas, all with their own guards and defensive positions. It wouldn't help them to have all of their stores in one area, in case they were over-run or were set on fire. The people inventorying the trucks had found another truck bound for the Jade Helm exercises, and it was parked outside the jail, under guard. At this point, he wouldn't be surprised at what they found inside.

The food trucks were also parsed out to three different distribution points near the Agency. With some luck, as Martha and the elder women had pointed out, they had enough food for a year if they supplemented with fish, game, managed their beef herds, dug roots and gathered berries. They were talking about a massive planting campaign soon, and teaching the old ways.

Martin came in and briefed him and the other command staff on the murders. "We won't forget this when we are back to normal," Martin said, a fierce look in his eyes.

"We're better off than most, from what we are hearing on the radio," Smokey said. "The cities are complete anarchy, death on every block for those who venture outside, including Madras, Bend, and the larger cities like Portland and Seattle. I can't imagine what New York must be like. People were dumpster diving in New Jersey on day two after Hurricane Sandy a few years ago. No one stores food anymore, or grows it. This country is in trouble. Whoever did this knew what they were doing."

"But you have to know, people are coming for us," Martin said. "People are coming for us right here, and it's up to us to stop them."

"We have to hold the bridge and the river," Smokey said. "If the north can hold for a time, with reinforcements going to George and his people, we can deal with Simnasho a little later."

"It's a plan," Martin said.

As Martin left, Smokey knew that the best plans go to shit as soon as the first shot was fired. Or in this case, after they were challenged in force at the river. That's where the assault would come from. Coming down the hill on the four-mile grade, four lane state highway – a steep bluff to the east, the river to the west . . . and then the bridge onto the sovereign land of the Cold River Indian Reservation of Oregon.

Smokey thought they would have a few days to get ready for the assault that was sure to come.

They didn't.

DAY FOUR

"There is an old Oklahoma Indian saying – *A starving man will eat with the wolf.*

I think we have starving people in the form of wolves at our doors."

- Chairman Bluefeathers to Jefferson County Sheriff Jimmy Asher

Chapter 33

Pelton Dam, Cold River Indian Reservation, 12:30 a.m.

Smokey lay over the fender of the Tahoe, looking across the dam to the Oregon side. He pulled the night vision binoculars up and the rock wall on the other side came into focus. Nothing. They had been waiting for thirty minutes and there was no movement yet. The chairman would be getting anxious.

He had spent the day organizing the militia and putting patrols together with a unified chain of command. With the help of Sergeant Lamebull and people from Natural Resources he had assigned people to guard the trucks, the longhouse, the administration center, the community center, and the federal complex on the hill. The militia had formed a group to go and reinforce George Wolfhead in the north.

Smokey wasn't completely sure about Wolfhead. He listened to what Lori and Nicole had to say, and he made George Wolfhead the Commander of the Northern Forces. He had given him a directive – keep those assholes contained or kill them.

Smokey pulled the binoculars down. He had a contingency of officers, NGT and others along the river in the dark, down the Highway 97 Bridge where the highway entered Cold River. The bridge was blocked with heavy equipment, and well guarded. Bluefeathers had given his approval for this meeting, and Jimmy was late.

When they had arrived at the dam it was almost pitch black, but in the last thirty minutes the high cloud cover had broken somewhat, and they had a little starlight to see by.

"Movement on Simtustus Road," an officer called on the radio. The road was downriver, and was in view for about a mile.

"What is it?" Smokey said quietly in his radio.

"We don't have night vision, but I think three vehicles, running fast, running dark."

"Roger." Smokey put up his binoculars, and as the other side came into focus, he saw them coming at what seemed an impossible speed right up to the turn onto the dam. Two black Suburban's, followed by a pickup truck. They were running lights out, and had their brake lights disabled. Running dark, for sure. The lead Suburban made a U-turn before the dam road, and parked. The pickup did the same. There was something strange about them, but Smokey couldn't tell what it was.

Smart, setting up a defensive position. Knowing Jimmy, he's got some heavy hitters in those vehicles.

The middle black Suburban continued on, coming slowly across the dam. The Suburban pulled up in front of Smokey's vehicle, and sat for a moment. The passenger door opened, and Jefferson County Sheriff Jimmy Asher got out. Smokey walked over and reached out his hand.

"Sheriff.

"Smoke."

“Thanks for coming, Bluefeathers is in the conference room of the offices above the reregulation dam, all blacked out. We can have you there in two minutes.”

Jimmy held up his hand. Wait one. He spoke quietly into his radio, and then told Smokey, “Let’s do it.” He walked over to Martin and Nicole, who were waiting by Smokey’s Tahoe.

“Chief Andrews.” He looked at Nicole. “This must be the pilot, Weasel’s woman. Welcome to living the dream here in Central Oregon.”

“Hi, Sheriff. We talked the other day as we flew over.”

Asher got into the back seat and they took off downriver, leaving his Suburban by the dam. It was turning around as they left.

Smokey knew what was different. The vehicles were covered in mud, twigs, sagebrush. A crude but effective method of camouflage.

He parked in the lot and they walked single file in the dark and into the foyer of the offices and conference room, a modern brick and rock building setting alone on the hillside above the dam. Smokey closed the door and they were in total darkness, and then a dim light came on.

“The conference room is brighter, thought we would adjust a little at a time.”

“We appreciate this, Smokey, don’t think we don’t, but my guys are very nervous, we are fired on every time we come and go from the police compound.”

Smokey nodded. As the lights slowly came up and he got a good look at Jimmy, what he saw shocked him, although when he thought about it later, it shouldn’t have.

"Jimmy, you've . . . "

"Yeah, the crisp look is gone, that's for sure." Jimmy looked down at himself, gave Smokey a grim smile.

Well, Smokey thought, *I guess we all look like that, but seeing Jimmy somehow makes this as real on the other side as here. Smokey had never seen Sheriff Jimmy Asher in anything but a crisp starched uniform, every line perfect. There were times he had seen the sheriff out in uniform without a gun. Mayberry. Jimmy now wore a dirty uniform the right sleeve ripped almost off, the lower arm bloody. His face was black and had bruises. He wore Battle Dress Utility pants that were ripped and covered with dirt. He had a load bearing tactical vest on, with AR magazines filling the pouches. He had a short barreled M4 rifle slung over his shoulder with a sixty round Magpul magazine. The rifle was fitted with a suppressor. He still had the same smile, although a little grim.*

"Chairman's ready," Martin said, and they filed into the conference room. The lights were brighter in here, the windows covered with heavy blankets. Chairman Bluefeathers walked over to greet the sheriff. Part of the reservation was technically in Jefferson County, and the sheriff had jurisdiction over non-Indians who committed crimes there. The chairman and the sheriff knew each other fairly well.

"Jimmy, you are our guest, and we are honored with your presence here." The chairman was slight in stature but there was no doubt about who was the most powerful person in the room. He wore a buckskin shirt with beads and his usual jeans and cowboy boots. Smokey noticed that he had his old service revolver in a belt holster.

Bluefeathers leaned close to Sheriff Asher and embraced him, and said, “Jimmy Asher my friend, you are always welcome in our land.”

“The honor is mine, Chairman Bluefeathers.”

Bluefeathers waved to a chair. “Jimmy, you are our guest, please sit and tell us what is happening up there in Madras.”

Smokey stood in the corner and listened.

“As I’m sure Weasel and Nicole reported, the center to the south end of Madras is total anarchy. There seems to be a group who controls most of the land there, and they kill everyone and everything in that area. We don’t know who leads them yet, but they are completely ruthless. They travel around on a couple of D-6 bulldozers. We have run up against them twice, took casualties.”

“What about where you are?” Bluefeathers asked.

“We have two hundred seventeen people. Some are families who made their way to our complex, some of my staff, several tribal members with their families, the Running Fox, the Johnsons. They don’t want to try to make their way home. We brought three with us, John White Eagle, Ronnie Smith, and Jason Harding.”

“Where are they now?”

“With my men, they will walk across when we’re done.”

“What about food?” Bluefeathers asked.

The old devil knows why the sheriff is here after all, Smokey thought.

"That's why we came over," Jimmy said. "I won't kid you. We can't even control the airport, the marauders take it over every night, and the nearest hanger is only a hundred yards away. My compound at the jail and correctional center is pretty secure, we have water, but we are almost out of food and medicine. We'll be losing people soon, some will run out into no man's land and die. I came here to make an appeal, and a proposal. We help each other."

Smokey watched as Bluefeathers nodded. Once.

"We propose to protect your integrity as a nation from our side. If you are attacked, and we believe you will be, we will take them on from the flank. But they are coming. And we need food, or we'll all be dead within a month."

"How can we help you? We are a poor reservation." Bluefeathers held his hands out.

"You have over a hundred semi's. All we want for now is one full of food, say, a Safeway truck." Bluefeathers pointed at Smokey.

Smokey pushed off from the wall where he had been leaning. "Yes, we have some trucks, Jimmy, but how do you know that for sure?"

"We have four of the drivers, and two who were hijacked and made their way to us. We calculated how many you might have." Jimmy looked at his radio, and spoke into his microphone. He looked at Smokey.

"Gotta go soon, we have aggressors at the compound. We will have to fight our way back. And consider this – if we know that you have trucks, the hungry gangs of people from here to Bend will figure it out as well." He stood and reached out to Bluefeathers. The tribal leader stood and shook hands with the sheriff.

"We will help you no matter what, Chairman Bluefeathers. Part of the reservation is also in Jefferson County. You are my people as well. Most of you voted for me in the last two elections. But we can fight better if we are not emaciated. I know how hard it is for you to give up food when you could keep it for your people."

Smokey walked to the door where Martin and Nicole were waiting. Jimmy followed them. As he walked through the door into the dim foyer, Bluefeathers said one word.

"Yes."

Smokey had known Bluefeathers a long time. He could still be surprised.

"Yes, you will have your truck. Here, tomorrow night."

Smokey rode back to the dam with the sheriff. He couldn't get over the contrast between the way Jimmy had looked all the time he had known him, and what he looked like today. Smokey had been in meetings and on joint investigations with Jimmy and his people for years. He now looked like a haunted warrior, no a haunted leader who knew if he went down, his people would most likely not survive. But he was a fighter, he led his people.

Who could have known that the starched uniformed sheriff with a boy's face would develop into this fierce warrior, and ally.

Jimmy and his men drove across the dam as the tribal members started walking across. The blacked out vehicles raced back up the road. Smokey knew that they would take the old trail through the Campbell ranch, then work their way through the farm country, and hit the airport at the north end, then race to the sheriff's compound.

He wished them godspeed.

As it turned out, it was one of the better deals Bluefeathers ever made.

Chapter 32

Above Simnasho, 9:30 a.m.

"So what do we do now?" Sarah asked George.

George was lying on his stomach between two trees, a hundred yards up on a hill above Simnasho. He and Sarah had parked a four-wheeler ATV a mile through the forest behind them. He didn't know for sure, but he had a hunch that leaders in battle usually needed to see the battlefield for themselves to be able to make decisions. The meeting with Weasel and his woman had left him thinking about who he needed to be. The respect in their eyes and voices had changed him. George had never experienced respect before. He had caused people to fear him, but never respect.

There was a pasture in front of them and then across the paved road, the Three Warriors Market was in ruins. The metal roof had come down on the burned out building and lay like a twisted piece of discarded tinfoil. George pointed at the longhouse, a block west of the market.

"They have more coming in. We need to kill them before they have a big city." What had started as a dozen cars in front of the longhouse was now more than forty by his count. People walked around the cars. A group of four men walked up the road toward the nearest house. He turned and looked up the road to the north. They had lost their crew defending that road and he didn't have the people to replace them.

He was trying hard to keep his emotions in check. He wanted payback, and now, but he wanted to act like a leader instead of a street gang leader.

"You ready?"

Sarah lay beside him, watching. She turned to him and smiled. "Have I told you how much I admire you?"

Her words took him by surprise. He hadn't thought of it much. Since Smokey had let him out of jail and he had accepted this assignment, he was just doing what he thought needed to be done. Sarah was his latest girlfriend. She was eighteen, he was twenty-six. He was in federal prison when she was starting high school. She had added a lot of gang tats, in some way to please him, to fit in he knew, had punk pink and purple hair, and nose and lip rings. Sarah was short and chunky as she put it in a self-deprecating way, but there had always been something about her. He never dreamed he would grow close to another person, but in the last three days, he had feelings for her that he had never allowed. Her loyalty, being right by his side no matter what the threat - that was growing on him.

He leaned over and kissed her, and the response was sudden, unexpected. Sarah began to cry, silently, and then sob against his shoulder.

George was still and then he relented and put his arms around her and held her close. She seemed to melt into his arms, laying there between the trees. He had a jumble of emotions that he tried to keep in check, thinking

That's your problem, George, you're thinking too much.

Thinking that they should stay on task. Sarah's sobs slowed, and then she pulled back and looked at him.

"I, uh, I just didn't know the killing would be like this, I mean we always talked about it, gang stuff and all, but this is real, this is on-going, and they will kill us if they see us."

George nodded, and then Sarah was pulling at his jeans. He started to move her hands away and she stopped him and continued to undo his belt. She gave him a sad smile.

"Come on, big tough warrior, take your woman."

"Right here?"

"Sure, it's kinda like, 'in your face' to those buttholes down there. Besides, we both need each other right now."

He started to say he didn't, and thought better of it. And they made love there, between the trees, a hundred yards from the burned out store – a hundred yards from their enemies.

It was more tender than he had ever imagined sex could be, although he had to admit, it was making love, a concept foreign to him. He pulled his jeans back on, helped Sarah with her camo BDU's, and saw that she couldn't stop smiling.

He smiled.

"You ready for this, then ready to run, Little One?"

She nodded, a crooked grin on her face.

"Sure, soon as my legs quit shaking."

He laughed, a low chuckle, and pulled her close. He realized that he was smiling as well. George turned around on his stomach, settled into a solid prone position to look at the enemy through his scope. The group of four had turned around and were walking back to the store. They were all carrying rifles of some sort. Enemy combatants.

George found the lead one in his sights, a bearded man wearing a dirty white “wife-beater” tank top, centered high on his chest, and pulled the trigger. The man went down in a spray of blood, and George began to methodically take down the rest. Sarah was shooting beside him. George dropped the last one as he reached the front door of the longhouse. Sarah was spraying the front of the building. Suppression fire, as he had talked about.

As the last one went down, George jumped up on the rock, stood in plain sight of the longhouse and raised his rifle above his head.

“Aiyeeee,” he screamed, the volume and strength of his yell carrying across the valley, surprising him in its intensity. He screamed again.

“We’re coming for you, you motherfuckers!” He pulled his rifle down and began to methodically fire on the cars, trucks, and vans in front of the longhouse until his rifle bolt locked back. Empty. He looked down at Sarah. She was reloading her rifle, as he had taught her.

Amazing. That we should be here fighting for our land. Fighting for my asam (wife). It sounds right, George, and you know it. Asam. What the hell is happening to me?

A bullet from below slapped into the tree beside him. He jumped down from the rock.

"Sarah!" She was turning to run, and stopped.

"Sarah, I want to tell you something."

"Don't you think we should beat feet outta here?"

"Yeah, but this is important."

"So is staying alive, my *atauwit*."

He leaned close, as another bullet hit the rock he had been on. "Sarah, I love you."

He was smiling as he said it, and leaned down to kiss her. A single tear slipped down her face, but she was grinning.

"Was that so hard, big warrior."

"Just wanted you to know." He kissed her and gave her a hug, as a group of shots hit the trees on either side of them. She took his hand and put it on her ass and said, "Try to keep this in sight and you can have it again." Sarah turned and ran up the hill through the trees. George ran, trying to keep up. After a minute, he just wanted to keep her in sight.

Damn, that girl is faster than she looks.

Sarah was saying something as she ran.

". . . more where that came from old man." She laughed as she ran.

They stopped a mile away, breathing hard. The trees made bright splashes of green in the sun, like blades of new grass in the spring. George turned to Sarah, and this time it was he who pulled at her pants. She took their rifles and leaned them against a tree as George took her clothes off. Sarah lay down in the grass and watched as he removed his clothes.

She reached up for him as he came to her.

George Wolfhead, tribal member, former federal prisoner, street gang leader, felt the sun on his back as he made caring, unconditional love, for the first time in his life. His *asam.*

Through her tears, Sarah cried his name over and over. They lay there for a while and then George finally said, "Maybe we should get going." Sarah nodded. She slowly released her grip. George laughed as they dressed.

"What's so funny, warrior of mine."

"I was wondering how much I'm going to have to trade for you, tradition and all. To your family."

Sarah's face wrinkled up and George thought she was going to cry again. Instead she whispered, "All you got, big man."

He kissed her and thought for the second time today – what the hell's happening to me? When they were dressed, he slung both rifles and carried Sarah down the hill.

Chapter 33

Hwy 3 Roadblock

When George and Sarah arrived back at their camp there were a dozen reinforcements waiting for them. The kids were sitting on the rocks with the Indian Head canyon at their backs.

They're younger than Sarah. Well, Anthony won't be the youngest now.

George knew most of the replacements, or knew their families. They carried short barreled M4 automatic carbines. Pockets bulged with thirty round magazines. George wondered about the guns, but that could wait. They looked scared, and then he realized how he must look to the kids. His body was covered with tattoos with streaks of blood on his face.

"Do you guys have a leader, someone you report to?"

A kid with spiked hair and nose ring raised his hand.

"You one of the Couer d' Alenes?"

"Yes, Gopher."

"You related to Martha Couer d' Alenes?"

"Yes, I'm her grandson. I brought some of my friends. Some are in high school and some work with me down at admin. Smokey told me to report to The Commander of the Northern Forces." Gopher pointed at George. "You."

Commander of the Northern Forces. Me?

Sarah hugged his arm and George couldn't help himself - he looked down at her and smiled.

There were seven young men and four girls. An older man was with them, a Šiyápu. He was about forty, short, balding.

"Who are you?"

"My name is Steve Brooks. I worked in finance. I don't know how to fight, but I can learn, and I just wanted to help the kids. Gopher is in charge . . . I'm good with that."

"Mr. Brooks is good with plans," one of the younger kids said, and he laughed. "He will help us."

"Okay," George said. "Here is what you will face, and it is deadly." He started to draw a picture in the dirt and looked up at each of them. They were watching intently.

"Block the road, but if they come for you run into the woods to fight again. Have an escape plan. You'll have to go up there cross country, use your four-wheelers. You have new weapons."

Brooks spoke up. "Smokey outfitted us with rifles and ammunition and some food and water. We have a van for you with more rifles, and some rockets."

George raised his eyebrows at that. "Rockets?"

Steve Brooks and the others led George and his group to a van. Gopher pulled out a box and removed a green tube, about four feet long.

"An AT4 rocket. Smokey showed us how to use them. Said they were good for about five hundred yards."

George grinned for the second time that day. Sarah was the first. Some things, he had been told, were almost as good as sex. This was going to be one of those things. With Sarah holding on his arm, he watched as Gopher demonstrated how to line up the rocket, hold down the safety, and fire. He handed the rocket to George. He tried the sights and then handed the rocket to Sarah. She struggled with the weight, then got it up on her shoulder and lined it up. She smiled and nodded, and George lifted it off.

"Gather around, folks," George said. They surrounded him in a group. "When you work your way north be careful when you get close to Simnasho. They might have patrols out, but I doubt it. If you can, get a team of two or three of you within a couple of hundred yards of the longhouse, staying in the woods."

They listened. It was life and death.

"Just before dark put one of these in the front door." George grinned.

Gopher took the AT4 rocket and they shook hands all around.

"You can count on it," Gopher said. "They came for us at my *ala's* house. My friends and I, we're all Wasco until this is over."

George and his team watched as the kids loaded their four-wheelers and rode north. They left the road just past the roadblock, making their way across the hillside.

I just wish I could be there to shoot one of those rockets myself, but there most likely will be a lot of killing for everyone before this is over. A lot.

George saw to the distribution of the new weapons and went to help his warriors with supper.

Respected militia leader, Commander of the Northern Forces, that's who I am now. Why else would Smokey and

Bluefeathers give me the rockets. Respect. Something I've never had in the tribes. And I'm gonna keep it or die trying, and maybe that's what it takes.

Dying.

Chapter 34

Cold River Tribal Council Chambers

Martha entered empty council chambers and looked around. The council had been meeting all morning and she had hoped to speak before they adjourned. The talk of war was the only thing on the agenda. In just days the people had gone from worrying about where they would find food, to how they would survive without electricity, to worrying about war.

Every place she went in the Agency, whether it was at the Indian Health Services Clinic, the police department, or the community center – there was an undeniable pervasive fear of an imminent invasion. The conversation would stop and people would look up to the south, the mountainside with the four lane highway leading onto the reservation.

She knocked on the door to Bluefeathers office and he answered the door. The Chairman carried a short-barreled rifle in his hand. He walked back to his desk where he had another rifle stripped down and was wiping the parts.

"Sit, Martha. I'm just checking my weapons. Going over to the bridge tonight and help stand guard." He said this in a way that didn't suggest any other course.

"Don't you think you are a little old for that, Mr. Chairman?" She had known him since he was born, but always gave him the respect of his title. Bluefeathers looked up from his task and smiled at her, and then he was grinning.

"You are one to talk, old woman. Word is you killed a couple of bad people up there at your place with your husband's monster wheel gun." He laughed. "I am only seventy-six, just a kid. I don't move so fast now but I have been shooting the cousin to this M4 the M16 since I was a kid in Southeast Asia. This old man can still shoot."

Martha stood up and put her hand on his arm as he wiped the gun parts. He didn't look up. "We need you for us to survive, Little Brother. You keep your old head down." She hadn't called him Little Brother since they were kids. It seemed appropriate now. She left him there with his guns and knew that he would be in the fight. Hell, they all would be. Gopher had the revolver up north. She still had her husband's 44-40 rifle and she planned to put it to good use.

Cold River Tribal Police Dispatch center

"Jen, I miss you too, but I need for you to stay put, to take care of *Ala* and Laurel. People coming this way to invade and don't want to worry about you guys at the same time."

"What about you, Smokey? Don't you think we have a right to fight as well?" He could hear the frustration in her voice. He knew how hard it was to stay away and not know what was going on.

"Jen, I love you, and you have to care for our little one you are carrying, I know how hard it is for you, but this is what we have to do."

"I know, it's just . . . so hard. Your daughter wants to talk to you."

"Hi, Dad." Laurel sounded as frustrated as Jennifer.

"Hi, honey, are you guys okay?"

"Yeah, but you know I know how to shoot, and Dad?" She lowered her voice and continued. "Dad, you know they are coming down the hill, don't you?"

"Well, that might happen," Smokey said, "But we are ready."

"No, Dad, I mean now, they are coming on the grade, and Dad, they have boats."

"How do you . . . ?" But he did know how his daughter knew. She just knew things. And he missed her all the more.

"Okay, Laurel, I get that, I have to go, give my love to *Ala* and Jen, and I love you."

"Love you, Dad," Laurel said, sounding very unhappy.

Smokey put the headset down, and looked as the dispatcher was waving to him.

"The sheriff is on the secure channel."

Sheriff Asher came over the radio.

"Smokey, we have been monitoring the road. Looks like they're moving, just now, got some D-6 bulldozers, big ones, some buses, couple of dump trucks, and pickups, vans. We counted a total of eighteen vehicles so far. We have some of our people in the weeds on the south side of the Agricultural Research Center. The bad guys are staging on Highway 26. Eight miles from you. With the speed of the bulldozers they might reach you just about dark."

So it's on, just what we need. Looks like it's show time. I need to alert the reservation and place more people on the three dams and along the river. Damn. But you've been in war before, Smokey ol' kid. Yeah, but not at home.

"Sheriff, let me ask you something. Are they pulling any boats?"

"They have boats, Smokey. How did you know?"

"Just a guess, Sheriff. Keep your head down, buddy."

"I will. Talk after you take care of them. If you can't stop them, they will be after us next."

Smokey knew they might all die tonight, but Jennifer and Laurel were safe. Or so he thought. They were too close to the killers in Simnasho. Too close by far.

Gopher came down through the woods on the east side of Simnasho. He knew the hillside well, he played there as a kid. Cece was his shadow and had been so since the first night when his *Ala* shot those men. She carried his rifle, one of the new M4's. They lay in the same spot that George and Sarah had fired from earlier in the day. He watched the activity below. The parking lot to the longhouse was crowded with trucks, pickups, vans and motorcycles. Gopher picked a blade of grass and put it between his teeth and smiled at Cece. She rubbed his arm, and grinned. They were alive, young, and were facing the thrill of danger with the certainty of immortality.

He pulled the AT4 rocket launcher up and lay it over his shoulder. He aimed at the front door of the longhouse, held down the safety, and pulled the trigger.

The front door exploded in a flash of flame and smoke. The men near the door disappeared in a shower of shrapnel.

Gopher and CeCe screamed and laughed and ran up the hill, taking the empty tube with them. They joined their friends at the top, still in the timber. After a celebration of high fives, they started off to see if a group of teenagers could block the road to the north. A deadly, important game for the survival of the reservation.

They didn't all get to see the end.

Indian Head Casino

Doc Semington looked at the line of school buses lined up in the Casino parking lot, facing the border. There were people around the buses, people who would be needed to attend to the wounded. He entered the first one, and the driver, Kip, waved. He carried an M4 rifle.

"Hi Doc, we got five of the buses, took some stretchers from Fire and Safety, think this will work?"

"If you can get people to me alive, I will do what I can. Make sure there is a medic on each bus with all of the advanced equipment they can put on here. If we really get into it, we're gonna have to triage as well as we can."

"Been there, Doc. A long time ago, but I haven't forgotten how."

Doc patted him on the shoulder, and went to look into the other buses. He needed Air Life, a dozen more surgeons, and medicine. But in a war like this one was sure to become, he did what he did with what he had. He sighed, weary, and knew that this might be the longest night of his life.

Simnasho
Fire Hall Truck Bay

The sniping pissed Abnormal off. The rocket through the door of the longhouse enraged him. He called for a meeting in the late afternoon. “Tell the folks if they don’t show up, they’re gonna be in the cooking pot.” Mike and Rosebud left to notify the rest of the people.

There were almost a hundred men and women in the bay waiting for Abnormal as he walked out from the office.

“I’ll be quick. We’re gonna kill all of those fuckers at the roadblocks. All of them. Those of you going south will continue to the resort and kill or capture everyone there, and we’ll set up our new command there. For those of you going west, go across Highway 26. Any houses or farms or ranches up there next to the forest, you get to keep. Take what you want. Bring back some trophies, alive or dead.”

He swayed from side to side and took a swallow of scotch. He dismissed them with a wave of his bottle.

Chapter 35

Pelton Dam

This time they came out of the dark in force. Nicole looked through night vision binoculars and tracked the vehicles from the sheriff's office as they made their way into the canyon.

"They're coming fast," she said. Smokey watched with night vision as well. The speed seemed incredible for the narrow twisting dirt track. Nicole lost them as they went out of sight behind the trees of the old Campbell ranch. In a minute the vehicles would appear on the paved road that led down to the dam.

Jimmy brought three vehicles the first time. Now he came with five. They parked on the other side of the dam and drove into defensive positions.

Two vehicles came across the dam, faster than before, the urgency not lost on the tribal police. The sheriff got out of the lead vehicle and walked fast in the dark with two others behind him.

"Sheriff."

He shook hands with Martin and Smokey.

Nicole heard the engine of the eighteen-wheeler start up.

"We've got our own driver to bring it across," Martin said. "Then it's yours."

"I can tell you that if we don't get this back to our compound, we are going to starve this week. It's bad." Nicole could hear the desperation in his voice, and the beginning of fear. She could only imagine how he was feeding over two hundred people.

"Good," Jimmy said. "We will have two experienced drivers in the truck. We had to create a diversion over in Madras to get out here, and we're going to have to fight our way into the compound. We'll get the truck there or die trying."

"One more thing," Martin said. "We loaded fifty M4 rifles in the truck as well as ten AT4 rocket launchers."

"I don't know how to use the AT4, but I'm sure I have people who do."

"Roger that, Sheriff," the man behind him said. "We know how." Nicole couldn't see the man behind Jimmy but he sounded sure enough.

"One more thing," Jimmy said. "The staging on the highway is moving. We are harassing them, but they are approaching the grade. It looks as if they're coming for the reservation tonight."

"We are getting ready." Martin said.

"They have been moving equipment up to the old Agricultural Research Station on Dogwood Lane for the past day. We thought they were coming for us, but they have bypassed us for now. Bulldozers, graders, trucks, heavy vehicles that will carry a lot of starving killers and assholes with no redemption. They have stuff that will bust through roadblocks. They're coming. And Martin, Smokey, Nicole - we have seen the effects of cholera in the city, and we have found a carcass, the remains of a human. They're eating the dead."

"Jesus," Martin muttered. "This is fast isn't it? I mean, it's only been a few days."

"That's what we thought," Jimmy said. "We were so dependent on going to the store every single day. A fifth of the country is on food stamps." He shrugged.

Nicole thought she was going to get sick, but she had to tell Jimmy something, before he left, and she knew she had only seconds.

"Jimmy, uh, Sheriff," Nicole said. He leaned closer.

"Yes?"

"I am bringing a message from Martha Couer d' Alenes. She says to tell you that the Creator has picked you to lead the people from your side of the river, that she sees that in you. She knows that you will fight evil. That you are a good man."

Sheriff Asher's voice was shaky, and Nicole didn't know if it was from the news he just shared, or his week long lack of sleep or food. His voice was quiet. "I, uh, don't know what to say except to tell her that I will thank her personally when I see her." He turned to Martin. "Let's do it."

The truck started forward and slowly entered the road on the top of the dam.

"Will that dam hold the truck?" Nicole asked, wishing then that her outside voice wouldn't be so loud.

"We don't know, but we are about to find out," Smokey said. Nicole held her breath as the truck slowly crossed the dam. On the other side, they switched driver, and the vehicles took off, shadows, running without lights, the truck going through the gears up the road, the cliff on the right, the river down on the left. They waited, and when the truck got to the steep dirt road up through the ranch, they followed it's progress up the grade. Even though it was a mile away in the night, the engine straining up the road seemed impossibly loud.

"They will make it up in just a few minutes," Smokey said. "We swapped the tractor unit on the Safeway truck for the hottest diesel we could find. They have a lot of power."

They are gonna need it, Nicole thought. As she and Martin and Smokey and their group prepared to leave, Nicole heard a shot from across the river, up on top where the truck would come out, and then a series of shots.

Oh, God, Jimmy, go with God. And why did I think that? I haven't thought of God in years, and it's that little Indian woman's fault. Martha. Yeah, I've grown to like her, to count on her, but she's always talking about the Creator, as if He's real.

Well, Jimmy, Sheriff Asher I hope you make it back safe with the food for your people. I think we're gonna need you. Oh God, now I'm sounding like Martha. I sure hope this country survives, 'cause if it doesn't, Weasel and I are dead in a day.

THE END OF DAYS

“Everyone with us today is Indian. Our visitors, our friends in arms across the river - we fight as a family.”

- Chairman Bluefeathers, Cold River Indian Reservation of Oregon

Chapter 36

Cold River Indian Reservation, Dusk

"Movement on the grade." The speaker was with one of the units just downriver from Pelton Dam. From there they had an unrestricted view of the Highway all the way to the top of the hill, five miles away.

"Copy that," Smokey said. He was in the Eagle Crossing Restaurant, situated on the river, just inside the reservation. From where he was he could look across the river at the Rainbow Market and to the state park a half mile upriver. The park was a favorite launching point for raft trips down the Deschutes River. Another life, another time. He wondered if the rafts would ever float down the river, carrying vacationers in the hot summer months.

Somehow I doubt it, he thought. He could see the last mile of the highway as it wound along the river. The highway made a sharp turn onto the bridge, two hundred yards of cement and steel, and then onto the reservation.

The cement and steel bridge was new and would carry any amount of weight. Bluefeathers had ordered the bridge wired with explosives. It would be blown up only as a last resort.

"You think I should go up the road and take a look?"

Sergeant Lamebull grunted, neither a yes or no.

"It would only take a minute for us to run up there along the road on the reservation side."

Lamebull got up and that was his answer. Smokey jogged to his Tahoe and started it as Lamebull got in.

Running in the dark it took two minutes to meet the units upriver. Smokey looked through binoculars at the caravan coming down the hill. They looked small from here but he knew the lead vehicles, the bulldozers must be huge. They were followed by at least thirty vehicles.

He had seen enough.

He was joined on the road by Officer Pauline Shiffer and a group of people. They clustered around her in the dark.

“Pass the word around. If they put boats in let them get within a few feet of shore, then hose them down with rifle fire. No sense using an AT4 on a fast moving boat.”

“Copy that, Lieutenant.”

Officer Shiffer is so young, is she even twenty-one? She had her family with her, some with hunting rifles. One even had a hunting bow, for chrissakes.

Lamebull was in the driver’s seat when Smokey got in. Lamebull had been to war as well and they both knew how fucked up it was going to get. Some of those people they just met with were not going to live through the night.

When they got back to the restaurant, Bluefeathers was waiting. He had on a set of camo BDU’s from the Vietnam War. There were medals on the Chairman’s breast pocket. Smokey looked closer. A Silver Star and a Purple Heart.

The things I didn't know about my Indian leader. At five foot four the Chairman is the biggest person I've ever known.

Judge Wewana stood next to Bluefeathers. They both carried M4 rifles. Bluefeathers had a bag with thirty-round magazines. Judge Wewana stared out across the river, full dark now. The plan was to light up the bridge and the approaches with portable lights.

"Boats in the water, below Pelton Dam." Officer Shiffer reported, her voice high, cracking.

"Copy."

Another voice came on the radio.

"Smokey, this is George, Northern Command."

"Go ahead."

"We are under serious attack at all three roadblocks, we need some immediate assistance."

"We have our hands full down here, if you can't prevail, pull back into the hills and monitor them. Sorry."

"George out." And before he disconnected the call, Smokey could hear the former gang leader yelling orders at his people. Kids actually, but tonight they were men and women.

They walked across the road to their barricades at the bridge. They had dump trucks, road graders, logging yarders, and even an old Kenworth tractor-trailer rig on the bridge. It was hard for Smokey to imagine that anything could move all of the equipment, even a bulldozer.

Movement across from the State Park. Smokey brought the night vision up. The bulldozers were bristling with rifle barrels, a dozen shooters on each. The next vehicle in line was a dump truck, a group of fighters in the back.

"Smokey, this is Nicole."

"Go ahead."

"We are approaching the river, want us to light it up?"

Chapter 37

D&D Garage

It was hard to believe that this started less than a week ago, Nicole thought. She helped push the Cessna out of the garage. The usual audience was missing. Many would be out on the firing line.

They were getting ready for what might be their last flight. What had started with a night flight above L.A. was ending in a flight above the Deschutes River Canyon in the dark. They would be the eyes for the Cold River forces.

There had been a heated debate in the tribal council as to whether Weasel and Nicole should go up at all, to risk the plane and the pilots. In the end, Weasel prevailed, and they were given permission to go up.

"You fly over and back, and if they are getting too close, you come and land, or land up on County Line Road, away from the action," Bluefeathers had said. Nicole didn't know what they were going to see, but they would be flying in close. That was the plan anyway.

They taxied up to the highway, and the plan was for them to take off uphill, away from the river, so they wouldn't alert any of the invaders.

"Nicole to Smokey, we're up." They flew up the highway to the north, up the steep grade with three paved lanes. The Cold River Agency was in a valley. The attack was coming from the hills to the south.

"Come around to the west, over Round Butte Dam, and then make a run down the road to the river. Light them up, they're almost here."

As they came around from over the airport, Weasel kept the plane at a thousand feet. They lined up back on the highway and throttled back almost to a stall speed. They flew on through the dark, to the highway leading down to Cold River.

Nicole couldn't see. Weasel had on night vision, and he said, "Get ready."

She propped her door open, and lit the first flare. The heat, brilliant light, and smoke filled the cabin. Weasel said, " Now," and then he said, "Again."

Nicole started dropping flares over the highway, lighting up the path to the Rez.

As they got within the last mile, with the river on their left, the canyon wall on their right, Nicole heard Weasel take in a sharp breath.

Ohmigod! What the hell is that?

The Cessna drifted closer to the rock wall. Nicole swung her head around to see what Weasel was doing. He seemed mesmerized, staring at the road below. "Weasel, fly the damned plane!" He glanced at the rock wall, and brought the plane back over the road. The harsh light from the flares made stark shadows on the scene below.

This is Mad Max, Fury Road, right here in the high desert. Holy shit, the big bulldozers in front have cages on them with dozens of people with rifles. They are almost to the store, a hundred yards from the bridge. There were big tracked vehicles with blades in front, with buses, trucks, pickups, tractors, cars, the line stretched halfway up the hill. And they are all filled with people coming to kill us.

"Use your radio," Weasel yelled, and then they were over the river and back on the Rez. Weasel was bringing the plane around again.

This isn't eighteen vehicles that we were told about. This is an invasion over a mile long. We don't stand a chance.

"Smokey, Nicole."

"Smokey."

Oh God I hope they don't push our roadblock away.

"Smokey, the lead vehicle the big yellow bulldozer is fifty yards from the bridge. There are a mile of cars, Lieutenant. They are filled with people with guns." Her voice shook at the end. She had never seen anything like this before. And they had to be stopped.

"The lead bulldozer is almost to the bridge. Do you copy?"

"Yes, we see them, stay clear, we're going to blow things up."

"Roger."

Martin Andrews walked over and joined Smokey. He had asked Lori to be in a fallback position at the mill and in the end, she relented. They had a roadblock there - fighting positions, in case the bridge fell.

Martin looked up as the plane went to full throttle, and he heard rather than saw the Cessna flash overhead. He looked at the officers and others around him. Bluefeathers was walking up the line talking quietly to the officers and tribal members standing in the dark behind the roadblock. Some of them were as young as twelve or thirteen. When you fight for your home, there is no age limit.

"Chief."

He looked over to the voice. She came closer.

"Chief, it's Rita."

"Hi, Rita, I thought you would be with your mother."

"She told me I could come here. She's on the radio."

Rita. Fourteen. Her mother was the lead dispatcher. Martin had known Rita since she was eleven. She had her hair braided in pigtails. She wore a buckskin dress with beads that her *Ala* had made for her. She carried a hunting rifle.

We'd better win this. Dear God, we better win.

"Rita, keep your head down, and I mean it. Promise?"

Martin walked down the line in the dark. Every few feet he touched someone and said, "pick your targets, shoot at a person, not a vehicle."

He touched Lonny Winasha who had been a police officer and left to work in the mill so he could be home at night. A good officer and expert tracker. Long braided hair, weathered face, small stature, maybe five foot three. A fierce fighter.

"Chief."

"Glad you're here, Lonny." As Martin turned away, he saw that Lonny's wife and daughter were standing behind him.

Smokey watched the bulldozers make the final approach to the bridge. He had a dozen of their officers ready with At4 recoilless rocket launchers. He gave the order.

The first officer fired his 84mm rocket and it hit the bulldozer cab in a flash of fire and smoke, the explosion obliterating the cab and attackers in it. The bulldozer came on under power with no guidance. It stopped against the first truck and the tracks ground away on the cement. The second bladed vehicle was on fire and rockets were firing at the following trucks and busses. The noise and smoke marked the beginning of the war for the reservation.

Bullets slapped into the truck around Smokey and he saw three of their fighters go down.

"Fire at will, pick your targets."

Dozens of people streamed across the bridge, picking their way around and over their roadblocks. Some were going down, but not enough.

"Lieutenant!"

Sergeant Lamebull ran up to him, coming from upriver side of their roadblock.

"We have rafts in the river, dozens of them, maybe a hundred. Upriver. They are going to flank us. This front attack was a ruse."

"Get some people along the road." He turned to find Chief Martin Andrews at his side. "We're going to have to fall back to the mill."

"I heard," Martin said. "Bluefeathers says to blow the bridge." Charlie Mathers stepped up beside Smokey to say something and a bullet took off the top of his head, his blood hitting Smokey in the face, his eyes turning up and lifeless as he dropped.

“Fall back,” Smokey yelled. He ran down the line to tell people to go. Take the wounded. Leave the dead for now.

Smokey watched Chief Martin Andrews put a wounded kid on his shoulder and go to a waiting car. He had worked for several chiefs, and this man who had arrived on the reservation from the outside was the best. Friend, fellow officer.

An explosion on the other side of the river caused Smokey to stop and look across the bridge. That could only mean one thing – Sheriff Jimmy Asher was in the fight from up the hill. He ran to find Bluefeathers. The chairman stood beside the truck, unprotected, firing a long burst at the approaching swarm. Bullets slammed into the truck as Bluefeathers calmly reloaded. Judge Wewana lay in a pool of blood at the chairman’s feet,

“Mr. Chairman.” He pointed up the hill. “Maybe we can fall back and keep the bridge for now!” He was yelling, close. “We have to pull back, we’re being flanked from a river crossing. Let’ save the bridge, blow the charges in the vehicles on the bridge, but not the structure.” The chairman nodded and calmly fired at a man running straight at them, the bullets punching the chest of the invader. The man fell at their feet.

That guy looks like the math teacher. God I hope not.

Bluefeathers fired another burst and moved to help the wounded.

Smokey's earpiece came alive. "Officer Shiffer to Smokey." Her voice was loud, almost a scream.

"Smokey."

"We're being overrun, Keelah's dead and most of NGT, the rest are missing, I don't think – "

A hammer of full automatic gunfire came over the radio, and then static, and the radio stopped.

Shit

Smokey turned around and went to help the wounded at the barricade. There was nothing in the world he could do to help the fighters along the river. He had to keep moving. Things were unraveling fast.

IHS Clinic

The first bus had only six wounded, and Semington went to work. Two wouldn't make it, two he could save, and two could wait for later. He was well into the work when the next school bus arrived. Eleven. He yelled at the nearest person, an elder named Sammy, to get him some more help.

"I need Nicole," he yelled, and went back to work.

The next bus had eighteen. He didn't even have time to triage.

Nicole and Weasel landed by the light of two cars on County Line Road and taxied to a nearby barn. The plane was under guard. A car was coming fast, Nicole saw, and the driver jumped out as soon as it slid to a stop.

"Doc needs you now," he said breathlessly. "He says now."

Nicole grabbed the bag with extra guns and ammunition and they got in the car for a fast ride down the mountain to the clinic.

When they arrived, there was no doubt that the war was underway. Nicole heard firing from the border a mile and a half away. Bloody patients sat and lay on the floor in the hallway. She pulled on gloves and hurried to find the doctor. Weasel walked among the wounded. He talked, encouraged, and prayed.

The Deschutes River Barricade

"Smokey!" Chairman Bluefeathers was leaning over a figure on the ground. "It's Lamebull, let's get him into your car."

Smokey reached down and grabbed an arm and lifted with strength he didn't know he had. Sergeant Lamebull weighed at least two hundred seventy pounds. Smokey got him up in his arms and staggered toward the police car. Bullets hissed by his head as he shoved the unconscious Lamebull into the car and ran around to the driver's seat. Lamebull might well be dead but there was no way to check now. He drove down the highway the third of a mile to the mill with bullets thudding into the car. His radio was a constant noise. He heard a familiar voice as he approached the trailer.

"Smokey, Dad!" Laurel's voice came over radio, surprisingly clear.

"Go ahead Laurel." His heart stopped in his chest. Laurel, Jennifer, his mom, the people he loved.

"Dad, the bad men are here at the house, we're in the woods, going further up into the trees, Jennifer's firing and –."

The radio quit as Smokey reached the overturned flatbed truck at the mill. He looked at Bluefeathers. "I have to go." The old tribal leader nodded.

"Martin and I and the others have this. You go find your family."

They put Lamebull in a car waiting to take him to IHS. It was all they could do for their warrior. Smokey fled down the highway toward his tribal home in the woods, almost twenty miles away. Smokey Kukup had served three tours in Afghanistan. He knew bad stuff to do to people, and he was about to remember all of it.

Cold River Lumber Products

Lori and Martha Couer d' Alenes stood behind the trailer. The noise of the battle at the bridge came up the road to them. It sounded to Lori like World War Three. No one could live through that, she thought. She tried to hear the voices on the radio, listening for word about her husband. It sounded like the bridge had been abandoned, as well as their forces along the river. Dozens of rafts had forded the river upstream from the bridge.

"We are pulling back from the bridge, our fighters will be coming soon," Lori said. Martha Couer d' Alenes leaned closer. A pickup truck came at them out of the dark. The driver slammed on the brakes and stopped beside them. Charlie Two Bears got out, his eyes wild even in the dark. He helped some of the fighters out of the bed. Some of the wounded stayed to fight - people with leg and arm wounds. They stared at Lori and Martha as they leaned against the trailer and waited. Lori walked over to the pickup.

"Got to take the wounded up to the casino and the buses," Charlie said. Lori looked over the side of the truck. She shined her flashlight into the bed. There were five people there - Lonny had a bullet wound high up in his shoulder, his wife holding him, pressing on the wound, blood seeping through her fingers. Two others were unconscious, maybe dead. The last one, Rita, lay on the floor of the bed, her head on Lonny's leg, a neat bullet hole in her forehead. Her eyes were open. Her buckskin ceremonial dress was smooth, untouched by war. Lori stood on her tiptoes and reached over and gently closed Rita's eyes. Martha pulled on her arm. Lori was vaguely aware that there were more people coming around the barricade at a run, getting ready to fight.

"They're coming. We must get ready, Lori."

Lori wiped her eyes with her sleeve. She had been at the baby shower for Rita. How can we tell her mother, who was, even now, on the dispatch radio.

"Lori."

She allowed herself to be led back to the barricade. The dim light from a burning vehicle in front of them allowed her to see people. She felt a kiss on top of her head, and knew that her husband had made it this far. He kissed her neck and put his cheek to hers. *"Atauwit,"* he whispered. Loved One. Tribal Police Chief Martin Andrews pulled away, held her gaze, and moved down the line, encouraging people, checking weapons. He was joined by Chairman Bluefeathers. They both wore the blood of war.

"He's a good *Siyapu*," Martha said, looking after Martin as he moved away.

"The best," Lori said, close to tears again. She shook them off and checked her AR15 rifle. She knew how to use it, and she was about to.

"I never thought bad of you for that McGruff dog stunt," Martha said, touching Lori. "I thought it was funny, you waving your rear end at all of those stuffed shirt councilors and elders. I loved you for it, my dear."

There was noise on the road and Lori could make out figures running at them like a horde of undead. They were firing as they came.

Martha Couer d' Alenes, a revered tribal member and elder, eighty-six years old, stepped out from the side of the trailer and lifted her husband's heavy 44-40 rifle. The intense pain in her shoulders and arthritic hands steeled her resolve. She gritted her teeth and fought the arthritis to hold the rifle steady.

"Get off my land," she whispered fiercely, and fired.

***Cold River Running.* The story continues – spring 2016.**

Books by Enes Smith

Fatal Flowers
Dear Departed
Shadowland Survivors
The Serial Killer Chronicles (a collection)
Cold River Rising
Cold River Resurrection
Cold River Running
The One Minute Lie Detector

Author Enes Smith

Enes Smith relied upon his experience as a homicide detective to write his first novel, *Fatal Flowers*. Crime author Ann Rule wrote, "*Fatal Flowers* is a chillingly authentic look into the blackest depths of a psychopath's fantasies. Not for the fainthearted . . . Smith is a cop who's been there and a writer on his way straight up. Read this on a night when you don't need to sleep, you won't . . ." *Fatal Flowers* was followed by *Dear Departed*. *Shadowland Survivors* is the third book in the Serial Killer Chronicles Series.

Smith's work as a Tribal Police Chief for the Confederated Tribes of the Warm Springs Indians of Oregon led to his latest series of suspense novels, set on modern day reservations. The thriller *Cold River Rising* is the first book in the series set in Indian Country. *Cold River Resurrection* is the next book in the Cold River series, and the third book, *Cold River Running*, will be released in the fall of 2015.

Smith has been a college instructor and adjunct professor, teaching a vast array of courses including Criminology, Sociology, Social Deviance, and Race, Class, and Ethnicity. He trains casino employees in the art of nonverbal cues to deception. He is a frequent keynote speaker at regional and national events, and has been a panelist at The Bouchercon, the World Mystery Convention.

During Smith's police career he worked as a homicide detective, patrol officer and sergeant, SWAT supervisor and commander, coordinator of a federally funded drug team, and a police chief.

He teaches interviewing and interrogation to police officers, and gives training seminars on encouraging truthful behavior. He currently presents keynote speeches and training seminars on the subject of his book, "*The One Minute Lie Detector*."

He can be found on his motorcycle much of the summer, touring the United States. He writes every day, and when not writing he enjoys hiking, camping, fishing, and racing motorcycles.

ENES SMITH

53129033R00156

Made in the USA
Lexington, KY
23 June 2016